SILENCING THE SIREN

By

J.E. Taylor

Silencing the Siren © January 2024 J.E. Taylor
2nd Edition

For additional information contact:
www.JETaylor75.com

Cover Art by Cora Graphics
www.coragraphics.it

Silencing the Siren

A protector. A lost soul. A siren looking for salvation.

Kylee Paradox never expected to be a protector of humankind, but when hell's portals open and let loose the creatures of the underworld, she can't see any other way.

Armed with an ultimatum, Kylee has no choice but to embrace her new position as bounty hunter of the damned. Sending these monsters back to purgatory becomes her life's mission.

The only glitches in an otherwise noble pursuit are those who hold her fate in their hands. They forbid her from using her deadly siren song to lure the beasts back to the pit.

If she harms even a single innocent soul in her quest, Kylee herself will become one of the hunted.

Chapter 1

THE SIGN OVER MY office door read *Kylee Paradox, Paranormal Investigator*, but I was really a bounty hunter of unnatural creatures. Honestly, I never expected to be a protector of humankind, but when hell's portals opened and let loose the creatures from the underworld, I didn't have a choice.

It was hunt, or be hunted. You can guess which choice I made.

Unfortunately, the perils of being a siren royally screwed up that plan. You see, if I employed my voice to snare these monsters— which, for the record, would be by far the easiest way to send them back to hell—it would drive any nearby humans beyond the edge of reason.

I was told there was no acceptable amount of collateral damage, especially if I was ever going to achieve my salvation. So, I had to curtail my greatest weapon and fall back on the warrior skills I had honed over the millennia.

I was kind of a badass.

This era was possibly the easiest to navigate compared to some of the umpteen centuries I'd walked the earth. It was so much easier to blend in and go unnoticed these days. But then again, everyone was preoccupied with their damn electronics. Unfortunately, I had fallen victim to the same technology pitfalls.

My computer buzzed, and I swiveled the chair around, dismissing the view of the Pacific for my oversized cherry desk. I glanced at the instructions that flashed on the screen, clenching my teeth in response.

I hated Fate. She was a bitch of epic proportion, and this latest order wasn't welcomed in the least. I hadn't been home in nearly a millennium for a reason. Now, she wanted me to go back and hunt one of my own. A siren had taken hold of the waters south of

Crete and was making everyone within range of its voice go on murderous rampages. The latest nautical victim was big enough to make international news. A cruise ship had been exposed to the siren's song, and everyone on board was slaughtered.

I wondered if I knew the monster luring those poor souls to their death. As if Fate heard my musings, a name flashed on the screen. My stomach dropped as I stared at the display.

"You have got to be kidding me."

A swirl of smoke bloomed in the middle of the room. As it dissipated, the blonde bitch stood glaring at me from the center of the damned cloud. Standing in her signature ruby dress that flowed as if she also commanded the wind, Fate crossed her arms, looking down her aristocratic nose at me.

"I do not kid," she said. Her voice was about as icy as the Alaskan tundra.

"You really expect me to take down my brother?" I said, pointing at the screen.

A truly evil smile flashed, and I just wanted to smash that beautiful face in. She leaned on the desk, narrowing her eyes. "You will do as I order," she snarled.

"And if I refuse?" I crossed my arms. Two could play the snark game.

"I will personally escort you to your dungeon in hell." Her lips twitched from a thin line of anger to that of amusement. I never doubted this bitch enjoyed watching me squirm. "I know the devil has plans to punish you for your insubordination. After all, weren't you once his prize possession?"

Against my will, I shivered, and a rash of gooseflesh crossed every inch of exposed skin. The devil had kept me as his personal pet, his personal whore. When I didn't comply with his wishes, he kept me away from any form of water just for the giggles my suffering brought him. When I was nearly gone, he abused me and then threw me into a fish tank in his bedroom until I revived and bore aquatic demons for his amusement.

I couldn't imagine what the punishment for escaping his hellhole would be. I was sure it was far worse than my original stay in his dungeon. But was killing my own flesh and blood worth avoiding an eternity at the devil's hands?

"Would you kill your brother?" I asked, stalling, but the tilt of Fate's head as she studied me left me cold.

"What do you think?"

I thought she'd eat her own children, but I wasn't about to say that out loud. The choice tore at my insides, but I finally gave a nod. I had what was necessary to kill a siren. Neptune's trident was stored in one of my many hidden safes in my home on the San Diego shoreline. But the thought of sticking those spikes through my kin didn't sit well.

Maybe I could talk him out of continuing this insane plight. Convince him to hide, to lay low for a while, and maybe Fate would lose interest in bringing him in. I helped him escape when I had fled from hell and made him promise to keep under the radar.

He had kept that promise... until now.

Chapter 2

I CROSSED THE THRESHOLD into my sanctuary. My shoreline home faced due west over the Pacific. This property had been mine for nearly a hundred years, and the house that stood now was more modern art déco than the turn of the century mansion that I'd once built. It had been destroyed by one of those cleansing fires that sometimes overtakes the California landscape.

The sunset tonight did not elevate my spirits. In fact, it did just the opposite. It made me yearn for the shores of Greece and the sight of broken wood planks drifting alongside blood, staining the pristine blue waters. I shut my eyes against the memories, as well as the molasses-colored Pacific.

Trudging up the stairs, I crossed the long hallway that opened to the living room below and stopped in front of the farthest bedroom door. I pressed my finger to the center of the doorknob and waited for the fingerprint to register. A panel slid open, and I stepped in front of it, allowing a scan of my eyes as well as the rest of my face.

The lock clicked, and I pushed the door open. The bedroom looked like any other middle-class bedroom. A four-poster bed rested against the far wall, along with a pair of nightstands. At the foot of the bed sat a large trunk extending the full width of the mattress. Along the wall to the right hung a picture window that had a built-in bench and shelving on either side, stocked with books and various knickknacks. The left wall behind the door had a long dresser that extended almost the full length of the room.

While everything looked like a normal bedroom, every piece hid some precious antique weapon, and only my prints, along with a surefire code, could open the treasure chests.

I stepped in front of the dresser and glanced at my reflection in the mirror. As forms go, the one I was cursed with turned heads no matter what I put over it. The less I covered, the more leers I got. My honey-colored hair fell in long loose curls, and I got questions about it at least once a week. I always got a cross expression when I said it was natural, like I'd somehow cheated the questioner out of some coveted hair secret. My eyes were the color of the Mediterranean Sea. I avoided mirrors just because one glance in my eyes triggered the sheer reminder of everything I left behind.

Fate transplanted me here in Southern California the moment I signed the paperwork. Of course, way back then, this was wild country. It wasn't known as the United States then. It was a tribal community of Aztecs and Indians, and I was a strange fit with my alabaster skin, blonde hair, and strange eyes. I think Fate did it on purpose. She wanted to see if I could withstand the scrutiny. I think she secretly hoped I'd fail and she could bring me back to the hell I escaped.

She certainly didn't expect them to worship me. I became known as Teo, goddess of sun and light, and that pissed Fate off. It was possibly the happiest time of my existence, and for a while, I forgot I was a fugitive from hell. It also gave me an appreciation of how special humans were. Their capacity to love and cherish exceeded my expectations, and it was then that I realized I wasn't put on this earth to destroy—I was destined to protect. It wasn't until a plague wiped out the natives that I truly understood just how fragile human life was.

I shook the thought out of my head and refocused, laying my hands on the fine cherry, pushing down on the wood grains. Warmth spread from my palms to my fingertips and back, then the lock clicked. I pulled my hands away and tipped the top of the cabinet to reveal an array of weapons. In the center sat the ornate trident, and I wrapped my hand around the cool metal. I lifted the heavy spear, careful not to let the tips touch me. While Poseidon's trident wouldn't kill me unless it pierced my heart, the tips of the fork would burn if they hit my skin while the weapon was in full form.

I closed the top of the bureau and laid the trident on the wood. Closing my eyes, I recited an old spell while splaying my fingers over the handle. "*Neptunus maris deus, fac mihi cessuros trident.*"

Light bled through my eyelids, encompassing the space in front of me like a bright ball of fire. When it faded, I opened my eyes and picked up the small charm-sized trident, clasping it onto my charm bracelet with some of my other deadly weapons. Since the advent of air travel, I've had to hide my weapons in plain sight. I just hoped they would allow this on the plane. Since the terror attacks in 2001, air travel had been more difficult to navigate with any sort of weapon. I only had one close call with my bracelet, but I got out of it by gushing over the trinkets and the exotic places where I retrieved the charms. Luckily, I only had to throw away one of the charms, and luckily it was only a charm and not one of my true weapons.

Without lingering, I turned and walked out, re-engaging the security system as I shut the door behind me. I stalled in my bedroom doorway. Normally, I was packed and ready to go on a hunting trip before the sun dipped below the horizon, but this time was different. I really didn't want to go.

I hadn't seen my brother since the last time I was in the Mediterranean, and that was right around the fall of the Roman Empire. Our goodbye had been bittersweet, and now the memory of that final hug we shared tugged at my heartstrings.

"I can't do this," I whispered.

Pictures fluttered from nowhere, littering the floor of my bedroom with death and destruction. I scanned the massacre, and when my gaze fell on a dead child, I gritted my teeth and closed my eyes. Fate's message slammed home.

My brother was responsible for all this.

I stepped over the discarded photos and grabbed my suitcase from the closet. When I turned, all the photographs but the one that got me moving disappeared.

I stared at the terror frozen in the child's wide, dead eyes, the scream forever cast into her skin. I picked up the gruesome picture and sighed. My chest hurt with the weight of it. Children, while enamored with the siren song, were not affected the way adults were. This poor soul had not understood why she was being beaten to death; she only knew mind-numbing horror in those last moments, and that fear was showcased in her death.

This was what my brother did.

This was what I had to stop from happening again.

I put the photo into my suitcase for a reminder, because I knew I would need it when the time came to go into action. Otherwise, I might fall prey to the hurt in my heart or the screams in my head telling me this was as wrong as it got. My brain went into automatic, and I grabbed a handful of underwear, not bothering to count out the number. The same went for shorts and tank tops. I didn't even match up outfits like I usually did when I packed for a trip. There was no rhyme or reason in my packing. The only thing I made a mental note of were the two bathing suits I put in as almost an afterthought.

With a mishmash of clothes thrown into the suitcase, I zipped it up without a second look. I really didn't care if I had everything I needed. I slung the strap over my shoulder and grabbed my passport and travel purse on my way out of the bedroom.

After dropping the bag at the entrance to my kitchen, I put my pocketbook on the table and continued to the refrigerator. Nothing looked good. In fact, my appetite had all but fled since I received Fate's directive. But I also knew a twenty-plus hour plane ride would leave me famished if I didn't force food down my throat.

Instead of looking in the refrigerator again, I crossed to the pantry and pulled out a box of toasted oats cereal and a bowl. I settled at the counter with the milk and cereal within arm's reach and opened my laptop. Scanning the prices for last-minute flights, my best option was twenty-one hours for three grand. That wasn't bad considering the other flights on the list were pricier and added anywhere from four to eighteen hours to the trip. I wanted to get in and get out as quickly as possible, so I gave myself a week to do the job.

I did another search for marinas on Crete that rented yachts. Many of them were only day trip rentals which would not meet my needs. The long-term rentals required either a captain or a crew. A valid boater's license was not good enough. In fact, it wasn't even an option. I banged my hand on the counter. I closed my eyes and took a deep breath before I scanned the choices. I sent a note to the Heraklion Yacht Marina requesting a boat named *Michael*, which only required a skipper. I bit my nail waiting for the confirmation, and when it came through, I jotted down the name and the confirmation code before sending a note that I required the captain to have sound-canceling earphones for the trip. Once the email was sent, I closed my computer.

If I needed more time, I'd probably get slammed with another charge for both the flight and yacht, but my bank accounts could deal with almost anything. Most people only had a lifetime to save up for a rainy day. I had over forty lifetimes, so my reserves were well padded. Besides, if I finished early, I would take a hit, too, because there was no way in hell I'd be sticking around to the assault of memories that the Mediterranean Sea brought forth.

I poured another bowl of cereal, thinking that perhaps a full stomach would ease the pain in the pit of my abdomen. I was mistaken. It continued, and now that discomfort morphed into an acidic burn. I tossed the rest of the food out and opted for a walk. After navigating to the sliders, I stepped out into the cool evening and crossed the road to the beach.

The roar of the waves drowned out my thoughts as I settled on the sand, crossing my legs as I watched the dark water churn and roll. The tide crept towards me. Even if I dove in, the ornate tail I once had would not come back. That was forever gone the moment I signed up for this job. Sadness engulfed me as I sifted the white grains through my fingers.

The sand shifted next to me, and Alex, my neighbor, took a seat, handing me a glass of red wine with a crooked smile I adored.

"You look like your favorite pet died," he said with a gentle Texan accent and sipped his wine.

Alejandro Cervas was probably the only genuine friend I had in this current world. He had moved into the duplex next door a few years ago after an ugly divorce that left him with little more than the shirt on his back. He didn't see his kids often, but he raved about them any time he got the chance. Despite his near destitution, he seemed to have the secret of life nailed down. A good glass of wine, quiet conversation, and now and then a cigar were all he seemed to need.

I offered him a genuine smile and shrugged. "It's been that kind of day." I took a sip of the wine and swished it over my tongue, relishing the sweet dryness of it before swallowing.

"Anything you'd like to talk about?"

"No. Not really."

We stared quietly out at the ocean, sipping wine.

"Anything I can do?" he asked after a few minutes of silence.

There were dozens of things he could do to help me get my mind off the coming days, but every one of them would end up killing this quiet friendship we shared.

I shook my head. "I'm going on a business trip that will not be all that pleasant. If you could keep an eye on my place while I'm gone, that would be helpful."

His smile returned, and he gave me a nod. "My pleasure, senorita."

I leaned into his shoulder, gently bumping it with mine. He bumped me back. After he finished his wine, he stretched out on the sand, just staring up at the cosmos. When his gaze turned to mine, the trace of a smile disappeared.

"Do you think we will ever be more than this?" His deep voice sounded soft and unsure, but the fire in his eyes was as clear as the constellations in the sky above us.

"Do you value our friendship?" I asked, because I could only forecast heartbreak for both of us.

He would age.

I would not.

His body would fail.

Mine would not.

I had tried this before, and all I encountered was devastation. My heart was guarded from that kind of hurt because it would spawn my voice and send me on a direct path back to hell.

Not that I didn't screw around when the itch presented itself; I just didn't make it about feelings.

He stared up at the sky, still contemplating my question. His rugged, dark features always made me wonder what his ex-wife was thinking when she left him. He had the same complexion the Aztecs had and the physique that would make a goddess drool.

"Yes, I value our friendship, but why is it so bad to want more?" he asked.

I cringed at the question and how to explain it to him. "I enjoy living here and make it a rule not to get involved with the neighbors." I couldn't help my frown. My rule was solid, but it conflicted with my wants.

He sat up, and as I turned my attention back to the water, his finger hooked under my chin, pulling my gaze back to him. His deep brown eyes searched mine, and just the physical touch sent my heart thundering in my chest. Heat filled my cheeks.

"So... no attraction?" The hopefulness in the arch of his eyebrows belied the light tone in his voice, and I couldn't help but laugh. Hurt bloomed in his eyes, and the trace of his smile disappeared.

"It's not that," I quickly replied. "You are stunningly attractive, and sweet, and..." I sighed as his hand cupped my cheek. Despite being ancient, I always seemed to get flustered in these types of situations. Especially when I was attracted to a man who could greatly complicate my life.

"Alex..." I started, but his lips crushed my response. Whatever protest I had been planning to launch died in the tangling of our tongues.

The way he kissed was decadent. He pushed me back onto the sand, sending tendrils of heat through my form. His hand slid from my cheek, down the side of my neck. The slow progression of his touch locked my breath in my chest as his fingers gently caressed the side of my breast.

The logical part of my brain told me to stop him, but the tramp in me wanted his hand to keep going, to find the spot that drove me to release my voice, to capture his soul the only way a siren could. I moaned as his hand traveled lower.

Alex broke the kiss and stared down into my eyes as his hand found its mark, settling between my legs. He stilled and cocked his head.

"Do you want to continue this inside?" His gaze flicked to our houses and back, and his lips curved into that sexy smile I had seen a couple of times during the past few years. It was a smile that immediately made me damp.

I lay on the sand fighting just about every emotion until he applied pressure with his fingers, rubbing in a way that nearly unleashed the siren song from my throat.

"Alejandro." His full name rolled off my tongue in a soft whisper.

He returned his mouth to mine. His fingers worked the button on my jeans, and I gasped when he slipped his hand underneath the hem of my underwear. Still, I didn't stop him. Instead, my arms wrapped around his neck, deepening the kiss as his fingers slid inside my wet core.

He groaned in my mouth like a man who had been underwater too long and had found a pocket of air.

He pulled away from me. "Your place or mine?" he asked with a voice full of the same need throbbing in my veins. He climbed to his feet and helped me up off the sand, but before I could say which direction, he had me in his arms, and his lips crushed mine.

I didn't even remember the walk back or the sliders opening to my living room. It wasn't until he stripped my shirt that I noticed my surroundings. There was something desperate and possessive about his lips as they moved from mine down to the curve of my neck. My bra released, and I tossed it to the side before I tore his shirt off. His chiseled abs tightened under my fingertips. I clamped my mouth shut at the vibration in my throat.

The soft cushions of the couch met my back as he gently pushed me down. His mouth moved over every inch of my exposed skin while he worked on stripping my jeans and underwear. I reached down and grabbed his wrists.

He lifted his lips from my stomach, and his mouth formed a surprised o.

"I can't. As much as I want to, I can't right now." The wild child inside me screamed her discontent, but I had to be logical and rational, and honestly, I needed something to come back to.

"Kylee," he whispered, pleading with his gaze.

"We can revisit this when I get back." I grabbed my shirt.

He dropped his forehead onto my thigh.

"I'm not rejecting you."

He glanced up at me. "It sure feels like it."

"Look, this job..." I closed my eyes and took a deep breath. "What I'm going up against..." I opened my eyes. "If I'm not fully committed to it, I could die."

His eyebrows knit together.

"And if I know I'm coming home to this..." Heat filled my cheeks, and I glanced at the floor. "Well, let's just say it's a guarantee that I'll come home." I forced myself to meet his gaze.

His head cocked to the side, reminding me of an adorable puppy. "What exactly is your job?"

I sighed. "I run a paranormal investigation agency," I said, opting for the cover story rather than the truth.

He climbed to his feet and crossed his arms. "And you expect me to believe that?"

We had never once spoken about what I did. Our conversations were more existential and less vocational. The skepticism on his face irritated me. I slipped my arms in the shirt and stood, staring him down as I buttoned up. He raised an eyebrow as I plucked the mace off my charm bracelet.

"*Hoc maior gratia*," I said, and the charm grew in my hand.

His eyes widened. I dropped the charm on my coffee table. The weight of the mace buckled the wood, and one of the spikes pierced it.

His ever-widening gaze bounced between mine and the ancient weapon. When he licked his lips and shifted his weight like he was going to flee, I crossed my arms. The motion seemed to snap him out of the shock.

"I'm going with you."

I uttered a laugh. *"Fac minorem,"* I said, and the mace shrunk back to the size of the charm. I plucked it off the table and put it back on my bracelet.

He stepped closer and reached out, running his index finger over the different charms attached to my bracelet. "I am going with you," he said again and met my gaze. "That way I can ensure you come back."

It was my turn to arch my eyebrows. "Excuse me?"

He closed the distance and pulled me into his arms. "I am not willing to lose whatever has started here. I'm going so I can keep you safe."

The absolute irony in his statement made me burst out laughing. He wasn't a god, or an immortal like me. He was a fragile human who had no business tagging along on a hunting trip like this.

"No. You are not coming with me. I'd be so worried about keeping you alive that I'd end up screwing up and killing both of us. I'm not putting that on my shoulders."

He pointed at the coffee table. "If you use that on whatever you're chasing, I'm coming."

"That won't kill what I'm going up against." I met his gaze. "That was just to show you I wasn't kidding about my job."

He held me close. "Are you a... witch?"

"No. I just happen to know a few spells that make it easier to transport what I need for the job."

"And how long have you been doing this?"

I stared at him, contemplating how to answer that. "All my life," I said, opting for more subterfuge.

He pressed his lips together. "And you've never gotten hurt?"

I rolled my eyes and tried to pull out of his grip. His arms tightened, holding me in place. He cocked his head, waiting for an answer. I was not going to give him a history of close calls, not with that overprotective glare now present in his eyes.

"Alejandro, let me go." I squirmed in his grasp.

"Look. I finally got the courage to make a move, and you seem to be on the same page, despite your earlier protest. And if there is a hair's breadth of a chance that you could get hurt..."

I stilled. "It's too dangerous for you to come."

"You realize saying that only makes me more set on protecting you."

"I don't need your protection. I need something special to come home to."

His grip loosened. "I need to make sure you're safe," he said softly.

The impasse seemed impossible to fix. I sighed. "I will be fine. Besides, you wouldn't be able to afford the trip."

His head cocked. "Where are you going?"

"Greece. Crete, to be exact."

He glanced at the suitcase, and his brow furrowed before he looked back at me. "Does it have anything to do with that cruise ship?"

The massacre on the ship made international news, and the fact that he jumped right to it made me stiffen in his arms. I opened my mouth to answer but thought better of it, clamping down on any response. Instead, I lifted a shoulder.

"Kylee, they don't know what killed those people. It could be some sort of virus for all we know."

"I know what killed them, and it wasn't a virus. That's why I have to go take care of it, so it doesn't happen again." I pulled out of his arms. "Now, if you don't mind, I need to get a decent night's sleep before I catch my flight."

He shoved his hands in his pockets and gave me a slight nod. He said nothing more, just turned and headed out of my house.

Chapter 3

MORNING CAME FASTER THAN I wanted, given I had tossed and turned all night. By the time I arrived at the airport, the caffeine had finally kick-started my brain. I made it through the metal detectors without issue. As I sat waiting for the airport staff to start seating the plane, I clipped the bracelet around my wrist and leaned back, closing my eyes.

The last thing I wanted to do was alienate Alex. The bitter taste of regret filled my mouth, and I swallowed, reaching for the bottle of water

I bought at the newsstand on the way through the terminal. I washed down the sourness and popped a piece of peppermint gum in my mouth, ignoring those around me.

I didn't have to wait long before the boarding call began. I got my carry-on bag, found my row near the back of the plane, stowed my bag in the overhead bin, and collapsed into the window seat. I glanced out the window and started mentally charting my approach to my brother. I was so absorbed in my thoughts that I didn't bother turning when someone settled into the seat next to me.

A waft of aftershave caught my attention, and I twisted to see who it belonged to. The physique of the man sitting next to me was as familiar as the aftershave. I met his dark gaze, and he offered me a nervous smile.

"What the actual fuck?" I asked before I could stop the words.

"I've always wanted to see Greece." Alex shrugged.

I closed my eyes and lay my head against the headrest. Whatever plans I had formulated all went out the window.

"Do you have any idea..." I opted to glance back out the window before I said anything that ears around me could pick up on and misconstrue. "I can't believe you did this," I muttered under my breath and sent a glare in his direction.

As the plane taxied down the runway, his hand covered mine on the armrest. I glanced at his death grip, then looked up at him. He uttered a nervous laugh. "I'm a little... anxious about flying," he admitted as the plane accelerated for takeoff.

I raised an eyebrow. "This is the safest part of this trip."

He gave my hand a squeeze but didn't say anything. Instead, he took a deep breath and closed his eyes as the plane left the safety of the ground. He paled a fraction and kept sucking air in through his nose and blowing it out between his lips until we leveled off.

His anxiety amused me and left me a bit humbled. I couldn't remember the last time anyone suffered through their own fear for my well-being. When his hand released mine, my stomach fell in disappointment. I glanced at him, sending him a slight smile before looking back out the window as we flew east over the vastly changing scenery of the United States.

"I have no idea what I'm going to do with you when we land," I said after passing over the Midwestern plains.

"I can think of a few things," he whispered. A dimple appeared in his reddening cheek, but he didn't look at me.

"Did you get a hotel room?" I asked. That dimple disappeared. He looked down at his hands and shook his head. "I was hoping you'd take pity on me." He gave me a hopeful sideways glance.

I sent a full glare at him. I didn't book a hotel room. I rented a boat for the week. There was no way I could have him with me. Not with what I was hunting. It was bad enough having a captain on board. One siren-psychotic man I could handle. Two would be difficult, if not impossible, especially when I had feelings for one of them.

"Alex..." The exasperation in my voice rang clear.

"I'm sorry, Kylee, but I couldn't let you do this alone," he said.

"I'm equipped for this. You aren't. Besides, I didn't book a hotel room. I rented a boat. And I cannot have you on board."

"I will be just fine. Besides, I do have a boating license," he said, sending me an endearing grin.

He did not understand, and I couldn't exactly enlighten him on a plane with strangers within ear shot. Instead, I glared.

"I'm not leaving your side." He stretched out in the seat.

Chivalry wasn't dead, but oh, how I wished it was. "I might just lock you in a trunk somewhere," I muttered under my breath.

He patted my knee and leaned over, planting a gentle kiss on my cheek. "I'm sorry if I have aggravated you," he whispered and then leaned back in his seat.

I sighed and glanced around. "While I adore your intent, I really can't have you on the boat with me. You are at more of a risk than I am." I met his gaze. "I know what did this. I also know what this thing can do to..." I bit my tongue before the word humans spilled out. "... to men."

A crease appeared between his eyebrows. "What is it?" he whispered.

"A siren." I figured if he knew what they did, he might back off.

The crease deepened, and his forehead wrinkled with confusion. Then his skin smoothed out, and humor filled his eyes. "A mermaid?"

I nodded and he actually laughed. He had obviously watched *The Little Mermaid* with his kids way too many times.

"You're kidding, right?" he said through his laughter.

I narrowed my eyes and pressed my lips together as the temptation to show him just how toxic a siren's song actually was to humans. But if I did that, I'm sure the plane would fall out of the sky and kill everyone on board, and I'd be the devil's plaything again.

"Sirens are deadly to humans. They poison mankind's minds, turning them into monsters. What happened on that boat was nothing more than a murderous rampage caused by the siren song." I chose my words carefully, hoping he would equate it to men, not all humans. I needed him to think I was safe on some level, and this ruse was the only way to do it.

His laughter faded as he studied me. "Will it affect you?"

I shook my head, opting for the silent response so he could draw his own conclusion.

"But it will affect me if I hear it?"

"Bingo." I pointed my finger at him. "Thus my insistence that you not come on the boat with me. It would be a shame if I had to kill you."

"How do you know all this?"

I glanced out the window, trying to form an answer that would hold water. "Because I have run across these things before. And I'm afraid the one causing this havoc was one I let go a long time ago. So, this is on me."

"You can't blame yourself," he said.

It was my turn to laugh. "Why don't you get some sleep? It's a long damn flight." I put the seat back and closed my eyes, avoiding any further conversation for the moment.

He squeezed my hand, and I squeezed back. Under all my angst, I was glad to have someone with me. Someone who could help pick up the pieces when all this was done.

Chapter 4

I DOZED, BUT EVERY time I wandered into dreamland, I shot upright in the seat with my heart pounding without recollection of the dream that caused such visceral fear. Luckily, my restless sleep didn't interrupt Alex. He remained softly snoring in the seat next to me.

I stretched, giving up on the idea of sleep for the time being. My shifting stirred him, and he opened his dark eyes, sliding his gaze in my direction with a sheepish smile.

"Where are we?" he asked.

His voice turned deep and scratchy with sleep. It was the sexiest thing I had heard in a long time. I took a breath before glancing out the window. The vast blue of the ocean met my gaze.

"Over the Atlantic."

He glanced at his watch and then bit his lip with a raised eyebrow. "How much longer?"

I did the calculation in my head. "Around another fifteen hours."

"I didn't think this through," he mumbled and got up out of the seat, heading toward the restrooms in the back.

I watched him go and sighed. At least the transatlantic flights had bigger seats than domestic flights, so the comfort level was better. I climbed to my feet and followed his path. He stepped out of the restroom just as I stepped into the hall to wait. He held the door, and a small smile pulled at the edges of his lips. I paused and met his gaze, tilting my head at the sparkle in his eyes.

He leaned close. "I can think of one way to kill some time."

I understood that pseudo-smirk of his and gave him an eye roll before slipping in the bathroom and closing the door on his insinuation. I did my business, washed my hands and face, then rinsed the sleep taste from my mouth. When I glanced at my image in the mirror, his idea surfaced, and my cheeks reddened with heat.

I shook it off and headed back to my seat. Alex slid out and let me into the window seat. He pulled out his tablet and propped it on the tray. I glanced at the display and then at him. He was doing searches on sirens on Wikipedia, a site shrouded with a mixture of mythology and truth.

"What are you doing?"

"Research," he said. "Not the best way to spend my time, but I need to do something so I don't have an anxiety attack."

"Why are you anxious?"

He laughed and waved at the surrounding fuselage. "I'm forty-thousand feet in the air encased in a tin can. I don't fly for this very reason." He reached into his bag, pulled out a bottle of water, and gulped down half of it.

I didn't realize just how afraid of flying he was. I reached out and squeezed his hand before rifling around in my pocketbook for a deck of cards. "How about a little poker instead?"

He glanced at the cards in my hand and back at the screen, outlining the morbid dangers of my kind. He folded the cover over the text, stowing it in the pouch on the back of the seat in front of him.

"What are we playing?"

"Texas Hold'em," I said, drawing a smile in response.

"What are the stakes?"

I considered his question and shrugged.

"We have to be playing for something." The cock of his eyebrow turned my insides into warm honey.

"Okay, then you name the stakes."

He licked his lips and grinned. "We can't exactly play strip poker on a plane," he said with a light laugh. "So, how about... sexual favors?"

His hushed whisper sent a rash of gooseflesh across my exposed skin and a quiver of excitement down my spine. I had to draw a breath to not visibly shiver at the thought.

"What did you have in mind?" It was my turn to be coy.

His slow grin sent a rush of heat right to my center. "Are we upping the ante with each card turn, or did you want to set what the winning hands represent up front?"

I glanced at the card deck as my heart pumped liquid heat through my veins. The safer way was to set the limits up front, but then that wouldn't be as exciting as upping the ante for each hand. I took a deep breath and met his gaze.

"We can bet with each card turned. The ante starts with a kiss on the cheek, and we go from there. However, the, um, mile high club is only available if you have a royal straight flush. If you call it, you have to show your hand. No bluffing." I figured the odds of that were slim, but if I didn't put the rule on the table, it was one I was sure he'd bluff about just to get me bent over in the bathroom.

His cheeks turned rosy pink, and he smirked. "Sounds fair. Wagers to be paid up after each hand?" he asked with a hopeful lilt.

"Depends." I glanced around the plane.

Alex scanned the sleeping passengers and shrugged. I guess the thought of someone waking up to find us engaged in sexual favors didn't deter him. As a matter-of-fact, his smile widened. I shuffled the cards and dealt the first two to each of us, then put the deck aside. I glanced at my first card and stifled a smile, forcing my face to betray nothing. The ace mocked me, and I bet on it alone without viewing the second card. I waited for him to weigh in.

"I'll start with a kiss on the lips," he said.

"Check." I cut the deck before I flipped the first three community cards.

The flop contained an ace, a jack, and a three, none of which were in the same suit. Now, I had to think of what exactly I wanted from him. My odds of winning with a pair of aces looked really good.

He bit his lip and looked from his cards to the ones on the tray. "I'll raise to a French kiss."

I wanted to see the turn card before I started upping the stakes. "Check." I grinned and let him cut the deck this time. I flipped the turn. Another jack. That made things interesting. I met his gaze, waiting.

His lips twitched. "Hand job through the jeans."

"Check," I said.

I turned the river. A three, which didn't help me at all.

"Oral in the restroom," he whispered with a grin.

"I'll see your bet and raise it to oral right here in the seat." My heart sped up just thinking about how taboo that was, but the thought of him kneeling on the floor lapping me

underneath one of the airline blankets made me
ache between my thighs.

He blinked at me and then glanced around
the cabin at the sleeping passengers before
looking at his cards. "Check," he said, his voice
cracking. He turned his cards over. He had a full
house with jacks and threes. His grin widened
as my heart dropped.

I turned my hand over, showing the ace, and
then moved it to reveal the other card. A five of
diamonds.

He swiped up the cards and lifted the table,
shifting in the seat with the biggest grin I had
ever seen.

I pressed my lips together against my smile.
Hell, it wasn't as if I had never dreamed of
seducing Alex this way. I just never thought I'd
actually be doing it on a plane full of passengers.
I threw the blanket over his lap and glanced
around to make sure the stewardesses weren't
starting their rounds. The passengers in the
aisle across from us were sound asleep. I
unbuckled my seatbelt and dropped to my knees
on the floor. He lifted the seat divider and put
one of his legs up on the seat and leaned back,
pulling the covers up to his chest as I crawled
under the blanket.

His pants were quickly unbuttoned, and the
zipper undone, leaving me with a view of dark,
tented boxers. I pulled his already hard member

free from his pants and cursed the fact I didn't look at my second card. But I couldn't begrudge him that much. I probably would have made the same bet on an ace high pair.

I drew his tip into my mouth, and his sharp intake of breath made me smile, as did the stall of shuffling cards. I thought about tucking him back in and taking my seat because, technically, I had met the bet. He didn't up the ante to swallowing, but I knew that wouldn't be fair. He won the hand and deserved a proper blow job.

The airline tray came down, giving me very little room to work with. His hand threaded into my hair, pushing me to swallow more of him than I was prepared for. I nearly gagged on the pressure in the back of my throat. His grip on my hair tightened, moving me in fast, deep strokes until his hips thrust, forcing his entire length into my mouth, along with a flood of hot semen. I swallowed and received almost a purr in response.

His body shook once, and then his grip on my hair loosened. When I pulled away, he tucked himself back into his pants and shifted again, moving so I could slide back into my seat. The blanket remained draped over him, but his face carried blotchy red patches. He met my gaze as I buckled in.

I wiped my mouth and reached for the gum in my bag, offering him a piece before I unwrapped one and popped it between my teeth. The mint explosion was welcome, overriding the salty aftertaste.

"Damn," he whispered and started shuffling the cards again. "I might need a nap." He leaned over and caught a kiss before he focused on the cards.

He dealt the first two cards, and this time, I looked at both. A pair of queens, but I didn't want to start out too cocky. It wasn't like either of us had issues losing. Most times, whatever the favor, we would both win. I just wanted the reciprocal action.

"Check," I said.

He stared at his cards. "Hand job."

"Check," I said, stifling a smile.

He rolled the three cards. Two hearts and a diamond, all low. My pair of queens seemed to be the best hand, but I wasn't sure I wanted to bet more than a hand job yet. There were two more cards to be flipped, and the sparkle in his eyes had me worried.

"Check."

"Check." He rolled the turn card.

Another heart. This time a six to go with the three and four, making the option for a flush a possibility as I glanced at my queen of hearts.

"Hand job under the clothing," I said.

"Oral, here in the seat," he said, staring at his cards.

"Check."

He flipped the river. This time it was the eight of hearts. A flush beat two pair.

I smiled. "Mouth and hands," I said, raising my eyebrow.

He blew a stream of air out of his lips. "Mile. High."

"You don't have a royal straight flush."

He turned his cards, revealing a straight flush, eight high. While it wasn't a royal straight flush, it was close enough, and I couldn't really deny him, not with that hungry look in his eyes.

"That's not what we agreed to," I said as he stowed the cards in my pocketbook and folded up his tray.

He took my hand, led me to the restrooms, and pulled me inside before the nearest stewardess turned around. Before I could protest, his mouth covered mine, and his hands wandered over my ass. He broke the kiss and dropped, pulling my pants and underwear to the ground.

"Turn around," he whispered.

I obeyed, staring at my reflection in the mirror and then his dark eyes behind me. He reached his hand around to my stomach and slid lower, finding my clit with his fingers. The slow circling of his fingertips drove me half mad. With his other hand, he closed the toilet lid.

I stepped out of one of my pant legs and widened my stance as much as possible in the small space. It had been centuries since I felt this kind of heat, this kind of connection with anyone. When his finger penetrated deep inside me, I clamped my mouth shut on a moan.

He wasn't gentle like he had been last night on the beach. His gaze locked on mine and was half mad with desire. He swept my hair to the side and planted a kiss on my neck, right on the spot that made me shiver with anticipation.

The moment he entered me, I thought I would lose it. The siren song made it as far as the back of my throat before I caught myself. I wanted this man. I wanted his soul, his devotion, his love. As we rocked together in the tiny space with his fingers and his manhood creating a magic in me I had never experienced, I realized just how deep my feelings for him ran.

"Kylee," he whispered and squeezed me tight, burying his face into my shoulder as he shivered with the force of his release. He pulled me with him as he sat down on the seat, huffing against my back. "What am I going to do with you?" His fingers hadn't stopped, and I arched as my body finally responded to his caress the way he wanted me to.

I clamped my hand over my mouth as the waves crashed over me. His soft chuckle in my ear brought me back to the present, to the fact we were in a bathroom on a plane over the Atlantic.

His hand stilled, and his forehead landed on the spot between my shoulder blades. "Now, I seriously need a nap."

I leaned down without uncoupling and pulled my pants to my knees. I wasn't ready for this warmth inside me to end, so I leaned back into him and sighed. "Me too. But I don't want to fall asleep in here."

He snorted a laugh and stood, forcing the uncoupling. "Sorry," he said when I whined. "I'll let you clean up." He scooted around me and gave me a kiss before slipping out of the bathroom. I closed the door and engaged the lock to do my business.

By the time I got back to the seat, he was already asleep. I climbed over him to get to the window seat and curled up alongside him, using his soft shoulder as a pillow. My eyelids drooped, and his soft snore followed me into sleep.

Chapter 5

THE JERK OF TOUCHDOWN shocked both of us awake. I wiped my eyes and glanced out at the Heathrow terminals. We didn't have to switch planes, but for several of the passengers, this was their final destination. I stretched in the seat and looked at Alex.

"Morning." He rubbed the slight stubble now present on his cheeks. "Did we...?"

I allowed a smile to surface. His sheepish question amused me. I nodded.

He exhaled and grinned. "I was afraid it was another vivid dream."

"You have vivid dreams about me?"

Alex chuckled. "Since the day I met you."

"Really?"

"Yes. But you and I both know I haven't been ready for anything other than friendship. At least not until recently. And then I was afraid of screwing up our friendship, so I didn't make a move..." He shrugged and studied his hands.

I knew he had dated in the last few months, but he never seemed to be interested in the women he found through an internet dating service. Some of his date stories were hysterical, but he never clicked with any of them. Each time he'd share a disaster date, I had to admit the outcome didn't disappoint me the way hearing he had a date had.

"What changed?"

"Something about how vulnerable you looked last night hit a nerve, and it made me realize how much I cared about you."

"So my vulnerability prompted you to make a pass at me?"

His lips twitched into a smirk and he shrugged. "I've seen you worked up before, and I figured if I was wrong, you might not be inclined to beat the crap out of me for taking a chance. If I was right, I figured maybe I could wipe that lost look out of your eyes."

I stared at him, contemplating whether I was irritated at his timing or humbled by his sweetness. I chose the latter and leaned in, pressing my lips to his prickly cheek. "That's sweet."

He blushed. "I'm glad I took the chance, but I really need to warn you. I'm not sweet. Sometimes I can be a little possessive and overbearing without meaning to be. At least that's what my ex told me. So, I'm asking you to tell me if I start behaving like a lunatic. I don't want to ruin whatever we started."

I let out a chuckle. "You mean like jumping on this flight thinking you'd be all hero-like and save me from whatever big bad I'm going up against?"

His face reddened even more, and he shifted in the seat. "Well... yeah. Kind of like that."

I patted his thigh. "I forgive you, but only if you listen to me when we get to Crete and stay on the island."

He bristled and glared. "And if I don't?" He crossed his arms.

"Then you will probably die."

His eyes widened.

"And I would hate for that to happen," I added, to soften his shock.

"Is there anything I can do to come with you and be protected?"

I glanced out the window at the airline hub. My gaze landed on the airman directing the planes with his orange cones and his noise-canceling earphones. I turned to Alex, my eyebrows raised.

"If you get something like that, it might work, but to be sure, I would want the combination of some noise-canceling ear protection, along with music playing or something, so there is no chance that if the siren sings, you'd be lulled to your death."

He followed my gaze and nodded. "I'd be willing to do that so I'm close enough to help if you need me. But if I can't hear anything, how am I supposed to know you need my help?"

"We'll figure something out." I wouldn't ever call him to action against my brother. Alex would be torn in two within seconds. The wisdom of having him onboard the boat was also in question. If the captain went homicidal, then I was putting Alex at risk. But then again, if I was fighting my brother, the captain could be used against me.

This whole situation was a losing battle. I closed my eyes as the new passengers heading for Greece started boarding the aircraft. We only had another four hours on this plane and then a short layover in Athens before the hour-long puddle jump. I honestly couldn't wait to get out of the stale air and get to the shoreline. I needed sea air. I could feel the dryness of being bottled in an aircraft for sixteen hours. It wasn't pleasant when I was away from the ocean for any period.

Alex's hand threaded into mine. Whatever color had been in his cheeks previously had gone. He looked almost ashen green. The unmistakable jerk of the plane pulling away from the gateway registered.

"I think my motion-sickness medicine ran out a long time ago."

I shuffled through my pocketbook, pulled out some gum, and handed him a couple of sticks of peppermint. He grabbed them from me and stuffed them in his mouth so quickly I had a moment to wonder if he even unwrapped them. His jaw worked, tightening and loosening as he chewed. A little of the green left his complexion, and he offered me an uneasy smile as the plane taxied to the runway.

"Just a few more hours," I whispered. He squeezed my hand. "Think you could, uh..." He raised an eyebrow, and his gaze moved from mine to his lap and back.

I laughed and shook my head. The noise of the airplane didn't drown out the conversations happening around us.

"It might take my mind off the, uh, unease pummeling every muscle in my body." Alex still sported a hopeful look.

"Not happening, Casanova."

"I know. I'm just trying to get my mind off..." His free hand fluttered in front of him as he waved at the interior of our plane.

"You want me to talk dirty to you?" I asked softly.

He let out a laugh. "That certainly wouldn't hurt."

I leaned close to his ear and whispered, "Mud."

The guffaw that escaped him was louder than either of us expected, which led to both of us cracking up. We laughed hard enough that he didn't really notice the takeoff.

When he started winding down, I added, "Grime."

That wound him up some more, but the grip on my hand belied the laughter coming from his lips. I turned his head towards me and planted a kiss. He drew a breath in and held it.

When I pulled away, his gaze locked on mine. "Maybe we should just kiss for the rest of the flight," he said. The clouds now blocked all views of the landscape. The plane climbed above the cloud layer and then leveled out.

"When did you figure out you were attracted to me?" he asked.

I met his chocolate gaze and sighed, thinking back to the day he moved in. I watched his bronze-skinned back as he carried his things from the moving van into his condo. He glistened in the midday sun, and the edge of his gray sweatpants darkened from the trails of sweat flowing down his skin. His bare muscles stood out from the exertion. I'd considered asking if he needed help, but I was enjoying the view too much.

"The day you moved in."

"So, we both have wasted four and a half years?"

"No. We became good friends." I glanced out the window at the cloud bank below us. "Besides, if we had jumped in right away, it never would have lasted more than a few weeks. I would have been the rebound. I'm not interested in being anyone's rebound. Been there, done that. It never ends well."

His hand relaxed around mine, and he leaned back in the seat. "Good point. But still, the idea that I missed the intensity we shared earlier for the last four years..." He shook his head and sighed. "Seems damn foolish."

"Well, maybe we will have a chance to make up for lost time." I didn't know if we would or not, but just saying the words seemed like the right thing to do. I certainly hoped to explore this further, despite my initial reaction on the beach. Yes, I wouldn't age, but Alex had quite a few years before he hit the standard of old. Perhaps if we made it out of this alive, I would tell him exactly what I was and give him the option.

If he knew the truth, would he still be all in like he seemed to be at the moment?

"What's going through your mind?"

I shrugged. "I'm wondering if you'll stick around once you get to know the real me." I closed my eyes and sighed at the fact the automatic editor of my words seemed to have been left back in San Diego. If I hadn't been a little sleep deprived, I would have never said that aloud.

"Kylee, there isn't anything you could do to drive me away."

I leveled a smile of sorts. "You may rethink that statement after all this is done."

Chapter 6

A THENS. I STOOD OUTSIDE the airport, taking a few deep breaths before I had to go back inside. The sweet tang of the ocean entwined with the air, soothing the dryness in my skin even though I couldn't see the water beyond the mountain range. The feeling of home wrapped its arms around me. I sighed at the melancholy that came with this homecoming.

Alex looked like he had been stuck in a plane for close to a day. His usual neat hair had become the bedhead look that most men spent hours cultivating. His long black eyelashes barely covered the dark circles under his closed eyes, and the bristle on his cheeks gave him a rugged look that I liked better than the smooth, clean-shaven cheeks I was used to. He took a deep breath of fresh air.

Being outside did us both good. The sea air bred life into me, and I was thankful to be so near my only true means of survival. When he finally opened his eyes, he smiled.

"I don't think I want to get back on a plane for a while," he said.

"We still have another flight left to go to get to Crete, but the bonus is we have enough time to grab a decent meal, and the flight is only an hour."

"Can we just stay put for a day or two? Go sightseeing instead?" he asked.

The way his brown eyes begged reminded me of the cutest puppy in the world. I almost said yes, but I knew a day or even an hour detour from this hunt meant someone else might die.

"I can't, but you're more than welcome to stay behind and see what Athens has to offer."

His gaze hardened, and his lips pressed into a thin line. He shook his head. "As much as you'd like that, I'd never forgive myself if something happened and I wasn't there to back you up."

"We aren't the dynamic duo," I said, rolling my eyes. I reached for the door.

His hand landed on my arm. "I didn't mean to piss you off."

I stopped. "You didn't. I'm just tired and a little hungry."

He nodded. "Me too. Let's go find some food before you jam me on a plane again." He opened the door and let me lead the way through the gates.

I decided on La Pasteria because I wanted a proper meal as opposed to getting my food at a counter like a fast-food stop. Although, I could probably stand through the entire meal after close to eighteen hours on a plane.

They sat us at a small table near the concourse, and I was content to people watch. When I glanced at Alex, he was staring at me. I shifted and tried to hide my unease behind a smile.

"How can you possibly look as beautiful as you do after being on a plane for so long?" He blinked and blushed after the words tumbled out.

His kind ramblings made my smile a little less forced, and I reached across the table, caressing his cheek. "I kind of like the stubble," I said, ignoring his question. I may look good, but the anxiety wracking my body left me with more knots than a bored sailor.

The waitress came over and took our orders. I got a simple linguini in clam sauce and a glass of white wine. Alex ordered chicken parmesan and a beer. When our drinks came, he raised the bottle.

"To exploring whatever this is," he said.

I tapped my glass against his and took a sip, thankful he hadn't toasted to the success of my mission. I wasn't sure I could drink to that right now. Eventually, I would have to tell him what I was and who I was going up against, but for now, I'd just enjoy my meal and his company.

Halfway through our food, he paused and studied me. "Do you regret what happened between us?"

"No. Not at all. Why?"

"You are unusually quiet."

I took a deep breath and gazed out on the concourse and the flow of passengers scurrying from one point to another. "I have reason to be." I turned back to him. "But this is not the time or the place."

"Are you okay?" he asked after a few moments.

Was I okay? That was a good question. Before we landed, I would have said yes, I was great. But now that I was here, too many memories seemed to resurface. I looked down at my half-eaten meal and pushed the plate away.

With a slow shake of my head, I softly said, "No."

He reached over the table and took my hand in his. Just his mere touch seemed to soothe the growing beast inside me. Gratitude welled up as tears that I quickly blinked away. But I wasn't quick enough.

"I'll be right back." He stood, disappearing around the corner. When he came back, he collected our carry-on bags and took my hand. "We're good to go." He led me out of the restaurant.

I let him take me to our gate, where he found a quiet, unoccupied corner.

"What is going on?" he said, his voice low and concerned.

"Alex—"

He put his hand up, stopping me. "I've known you long enough, Kylee, so please don't pass this off as jet lag or some equally insulting excuse."

I stared into his worried eyes. "I'm not sure how to say this."

He waited quietly while I considered my words. "What if you were sent on a mission to kill one of your siblings?"

He uttered a sharp bark of a laugh before the humor faded from his face. "You're serious." My slow nod answered his question, and he leaned back in the chair and glanced out the window. "I don't think I could do it."

"What if they were responsible for at least five thousand deaths, and if you didn't stop them, there could be countless more?"

His gaze snapped back to mine, and he huffed, crossing his arms. "I thought you said it was a siren." An undertone of sarcasm laced his voice.

The sting of tears burned my eyes. "It is." My words caught in my throat, and I wasn't sure he heard me because his expression didn't change. I cursed under my breath at the sudden swell of emotion. I shook my head to get a hold of the rising panic filling my soul.

I didn't understand why it was so damn important for this man to understand. After all, he was just a mere mortal. The plane ride had done something to my ability to keep distant. My mind drifted to the way he had claimed me in the bathroom.

"My brother killed those people, and I need to stop him before he does it again."

Alex leaned forward. "Why didn't you just tell me that? Why did you have to make up something about a damn mystical creature?"

Anger flared under my skin. "I did not make it up, Alex. My brother is a fucking siren, and I told him to lay low, but the idiot didn't listen to me, and now I have to take him out or I'll end up..." My brain caught my mouth before I told him I'd end up in hell. That was too much for him to absorb right now. His incredulous glare told me I had let too much slip. "I have to stop him before he pulls this shit again, and unfortunately, that means I have to kill him."

Alex slowly sat back in the chair with an unreadable expression.

"Really?" he finally asked and raised both eyebrows.

It wasn't that cute, endearing expression I was used to on the San Diego beach. This was a challenge with some dangerous undertones.

I had half a mind to show him just what kind of damage a siren could do. "Yes," I growled through clenched teeth. Self-preservation kept me from letting loose.

His skeptical gaze dropped to the bracelet around my wrist with all my little trinkets, and the snark in his expression softened. He sucked the side of his lip between his teeth, and when his gaze came back to mine, it wasn't as angry, but it still held a million and one questions.

Unfortunately, the concourse had started to fill up, and I couldn't get into this without strangers overhearing. It was never good to talk about killing someone at an airport. Alex's gaze wandered as people took the seats around us.

"We will talk about this when we land."

There was no leeway in his statement, and the warrior in me bristled. I never took kindly to being told what to do, but I let it go. He had a right to know, especially since he walked into a relationship with me without a clue.

Chapter 7

THE CALL FOR A flight interrupted our silent stew. I looked at my ticket and stood. Alex didn't follow.

"I don't think we are sitting together on this flight." He showed me his ticket, and he was right. My seat was in the sixth row of the plane, and his was in the twentieth row. A part of me was relieved, enough so that I ignored the uneasy smile on his face and turned, boarding with the premiere passengers instead of waiting for him. I was situated in my seat when he walked by. Our eyes met, and he offered me a terrified smile, trying to feign bravery.

"You'll be fine," I said, and he nodded, but I doubted my words did anything to settle him. Guilt bit at me, and I glanced back to see him slide into a window seat.

"Would you like to sit with your friend?" the woman sitting in the aisle seat asked.

"Thanks for asking, but he's a big boy. He'll be fine," I said.

"Yes, but will you be, dear?" she asked.

I met her gaze with a smirk. "I'll be fine," I assured her, amused by the grandmother's comment. I needed the break. I needed the quiet without that questioning look. I also needed Alex to noodle on his own thoughts for a while. Maybe once we landed, he wouldn't corner me and force my hand.

Even if he wanted to talk once we landed, we'd have precious few moments before I went out on the boat I chartered. I would not allow the man on board if he didn't have those sound-canceling earphones, so that was a detour we would have to take, although I had no idea where to procure such things nowadays. I had requested that in my charter notes, and I hoped like hell the captain heeded my request. Otherwise, I would have a rabid man on board, and my brother would be the least of my worries.

As soon as we were in the air, I headed back to use the restroom. Alex's gaze was locked out the window and his hands clamped on the armrests. I paused at the seat.

"How are you doing?" I asked.

His head snapped in my direction. His eyes were like saucers of raw fear, and the smile looked as forced as his voice sounded when he said, "Just fine."

I traded a glance with his seatmate and continued on to the lavatory. Something about leaving him to deal with his fear of flying didn't settle well. When I stepped out of the bathroom, he was there, waiting for the facilities.

He stopped me from passing and pulled me close. "If your brother is one of those things, what the hell does that make you?" He didn't wait for a response. Instead, he slid into the bathroom and closed the door.

Retching noises came from inside and I paused, focusing on him instead of the sting of his question framed in accusation.

"Are you okay?" I asked through the door.

"Airsick." Then he retched again.

I put my hand on the door, sighed, and headed back to my seat. There wasn't a thing I could do for him right now, and it looked like there would be no peace when we landed.

"How's your friend?"

I glanced at my elderly seatmate. "Airsick. He doesn't do well on planes." I leaned closer. "And he followed me here, so..." I shrugged and gave her a smile.

She gasped. "He's a stalker?"

"No, not at all. It's really more complicated than that." I glanced out the window. "I guess he just didn't want to hit the pause button on what we started before I left."

Her hand fluttered to her lips. "That is so sweet!"

I couldn't help the smile that surfaced. "Yes. Incredibly sweet, but not incredibly practical."

She patted my knee. "Sometimes those are the best people to have around."

I looked over my shoulder to see if he was back in his seat. It was still empty. I chewed my bottom lip as worry prickled my skin. I unclipped my seatbelt and stood just as he came out of the restroom. He smiled sheepishly. After making sure he made it to his seat, I slowly sat down again. The ding of the seatbelt sign came on, followed by the announcement to right our seats and prepare for final approach. I collected my things, stowed them under the seat in front of me, and followed the stewardess's directions.

The minute the wheels touched down, seatbelts across the plane were undone, and the passengers started gathering their things. For a moment, I entertained fleeing the plane and letting Alex fend for himself, but he would likely be foolish enough to follow me.

I stayed in the seat until most of the passengers departed and then stood to retrieve my bag just in time for Alex to stop and let me lead the way.

"I honestly thought you were going to bolt," he said as we walked through the concourse.

"The thought crossed my mind."

We stepped outside, and I raised my hand to flag down a cab.

"I'm not sure what to do with the conversation we had at the airport."

I glanced back at him. "Look, I didn't ask you to come with. In fact, I expressly said no for this very reason. If I'm worried about you, I'm more apt to make a mistake, so unless you want me dead, I suggest you table this conversation for later."

A cab pulled up then, and I threw my bags into the trunk and slid inside, waiting for Alex to do the same.

As soon as the door closed behind him, I said, "Heraklion Yacht Marina, please." I turned to Alex. "If I said I was, does that change the way you feel?"

He blinked and leaned farther into the seat. My heart sank at the torn expression on his face. He stared at his hands for a moment and then gazed back at me with the slightest shake of his head.

"So you've done some of the same things as your brother?" he asked, his voice soft enough for me to pick up over the rumble of the cab's engine.

"A long, long time ago, yes."

He paled. "How long ago?"

I chuckled and looked out the window at the passing scenery. "How far back does Crete civilization go?" I asked the cab driver.

He rambled about archeological discoveries dating as far back as seven thousand BC, but that the first evidence of pottery was dated between three thousand BC and twenty-five hundred BC.

I watched Alex's profile as the cab driver explained the Minoan civilization and the timeline of the rise of modern civilization. His gaze turned to mine, silently asking the million dollar question. Had I seen the dawn of true civilization?

In fact, I had, but the devil caught me before I could see the accurate measure of progress of the Bronze Age. By the time I escaped the devil's prison, the crude wood boats that easily smashed on the rocks had turned to more structurally sound wooden vessels. A part of me wanted to use my voice to tempt the sailors, to claim their souls and witness the destruction. I could only envision how those vessels sounded as they crashed upon the jagged rocks.

Fate had intervened before I had another taste of death.

Alex's pallor improved. When we stopped at the marina entrance, I peeled off the fare as Alex collected the bags.

"You look damn good for your age," he muttered under his breath.

I stopped and faced him. "Alejandro Cervas, you were the one that insisted on making a pass and jumped on a transatlantic flight in some sort of misguided chivalry."

He shifted and nodded.

"So, does this change what we started?"

He laughed and shoved his hands in his pockets. "I don't know. I'm tired as hell and need some solid sleep. Who knows, maybe this is just a bizarre dream, and I'll wake up with you in my arms in your house."

"Before you get some sleep, we need to find you some of those noise-canceling earphones."

He stepped closer with a crooked smile. "So, if I asked you to sing for me?"

"I would say no."

His smile disappeared. "Why not?"

"It would kill you."

"Oh."

Nothing like a death threat to ruin the mood. I turned and glanced at the boats. The only one I recognized was the *Christy*. But that wasn't the one I had tentatively rented. I didn't wait for any more of this crazy conversation. Instead, I headed toward the office to secure my ride.

Chapter 8

"WHAT DO YOU MEAN the boat I chartered was rented to someone else?" Frustration welled into my voice.

The bell over the door rang. I didn't bother turning around since I already knew it was Alex just by the trace of his aftershave.

"Is there a problem here, honey?" he asked.

I spun towards him. "The boat I thought I had chartered was already rented out, and all that is left is that one, which comes with a three-man crew," I spouted as hot lava formed in my stomach, spreading in the form of a panic attack.

If I took that boat, it would mean four men to contend with, not two. I was badass, but I wasn't sure if I could handle four siren-crazed men, especially if they were all as big as Alex.

"We don't need a crew," Alex said, looking past me at the rental agent. "We don't even need a captain, but I understand that's required." He crossed the office and put his arm around me.

"It's either that or we can offer you a day cruiser," the heavyset rental agent said.

I traded a glance with Alex. I couldn't afford to just take the day cruiser. I needed to go out farther than what a day trip rental would allow.

"Fine," I sighed. "But the crew is required to wear soundproof ear protectors for the trip, like I had specified in my original request."

"About that, ma'am, they asked if that was truly necessary."

Alex's arm tightened around me like a vise. Perhaps he saw the flash of anger in my eyes. I certainly felt it, along with the resulting pounding in my head.

"I'm afraid we must insist," he said.

The rental agent gave a single nod. "That will be seventeen thousand euros."

"Excuse me? That's double what I had reserved."

"I am sorry, but we explained it is truly first come, first served."

They had explained, but I thought I had been clear that I would compensate them for holding the boat I wanted. Apparently, this schmuck didn't get the message. I had no choice. Sure, I could've gone to another port and hope for a rental that would meet my needs, but I was tired and needed a nap before I headed to the last spot I saw my brother before Fate pulled me from the sea.

I pulled out my wallet and nearly threw the credit card at the rental agent. He rang us up and went through the regulations before waving us towards the boat.

I climbed aboard, and Faraji, the host, took our luggage and gave us a tour of the boat. He introduced us to Taavi, the cook, along with Captain Hagan. All three were sizeable men.

Captain Hagan cleared his throat. "I do not understand the request for noise-canceling headphones."

"Do you have them?" I asked.

He glanced at Alex and then back at me, nodding. "Yes. I have a pair for you as well, but I wasn't aware that another passenger was going to be with us."

I smiled and hooked my thumb towards Alex.. "He can have the extra pair. As soon as we clear the port, I would appreciate you all putting the headphones on."

"Yes, ma'am."

"I think I am going to take a little nap," I said with a yawn. "Please wake me up when we get to the south shore." I reached into my pocket and pulled out the coordinates. "This is our first destination." I handed it to the captain before I headed down to the cabin.

Alex followed and collapsed face first on the bed. When he lifted his head, meeting my gaze, I laughed.

"What are you doing?"

He opened his mouth and closed it before any words came out. Then he rolled off the bed onto his feet. "I'm sorry. I just assumed." He turned towards the stairwell and the second bedroom.

"Alex?" I said as he took the first step. He turned towards me. "If you want to stay, that's okay with me."

The change in his expression was immediate, and it warmed my soul. His smile brightened the room. He closed the door at the base of the stairs before crossing back to the bed. This time, he didn't just drop onto the bed; instead, he stripped to his boxers and climbed under the sheets, hugging the pillow.

I thought the man was asleep before I slid under the covers next to him. I glanced at his thick black hair and ran my fingers through it. He turned his sleepy gaze to me at the touch.

"You okay?" he whispered.

I stared up at the ceiling and then out the window at the blue sky, shaking my head. "I'm not sure how I'm going to get this done."

He propped himself up on his elbows, but didn't speak. He studied my face with an expression I couldn't read.

"How old are you?" he asked.

My eyebrows rose. "That's not a question you ask a woman."

A smirk appeared. "I know you don't go mermaid in the water, so what do you really look like?"

I sighed and rolled away from him. I didn't want to have this kind of conversation. Besides, I barely remembered what I looked like, but I remembered my brother. Mermaids and mermen were not Ariel or even that chick from *Splash*. We were scary creatures with voices like a host of angels.

"Kylee?"

I turned, meeting his brown-eyed stare. "Fate turned me into what you see, and I've been like this for multiple millenniums. I don't change. I don't age. This is it."

He ran his finger over my cheek and then over my lips. "It could be worse. You could look like that rental guy."

I burst out laughing. I couldn't help it. He joined me with a low chuckle.

"Come here." He rolled on his side, pulling my back to his chest, spooning me in his arms. "Get some sleep, and then we'll figure out what to do with the three stooges upstairs."

Chapter 9

THE SOFT KNOCK ON the door woke me. Awareness of Alex's light snore filtered into my consciousness, along with the continuous knock. I opened my eyes to the dark room, and every synapse in my body roared to life.

It shouldn't have been dark.

I pulled the door open with no memory of crossing the distance and stared into Captain Hagan's eyes. "What the hell?" I snapped and waved towards the dark room behind me.

"Neither of you woke, so we continued our heading and have set anchor for the night."

"You aren't wearing the ear protection." My body reacted before I could stop it. I pulled Captain Hagan into the dark room and flipped him to the ground, kicking the door closed and drenching us in darkness.

The light by the bed came on, and Alex sat up, his eyes as wide as the Captain's on the floor at my feet.

"Kylee," Alex barked.

"He kept going, and none of you have the ear protectors on." I stared Alex down until movement out of the corner of my eye drew my attention back to Captain Hagan. He was attempting to get up. I jabbed the heel of my palm into his temple, knocking him out.

"Are you insane?" Alex jumped out of bed.

I glared at him. "I have no idea how far out we are, or even if these men heard the siren call. I can't take the risk." I flipped open my suitcase and grabbed a skein of rope. "Are you going to help me?"

"Help you do what?" he asked and ran his hand through his hair, making him look much more harried than I felt.

"Tie the captain up so he can't hurt himself or anyone else."

Alex didn't understand the danger; that was clear from the horrified expression on his face. When he didn't move to help, I unraveled the rope and rolled the captain onto his belly, pulling his wrists behind him.

"Is this really necessary?" he asked.

But I didn't stop until the captain's wrists were bound tight and the end of the rope was anchored around the bed footing. "Do I need to tie you up?" I asked and stood.

He laughed a high-pitched laugh and shook his head. "Besides, I'd really like to see you try." He crossed his arms, cocking his head and giving me a crooked smile.

I stepped close, narrowing my eyes. He reached out, but I knocked his hand away. His eyes widened, and the smug smile faded.

"Kylee, I was just kidding." His voice was soft, his gaze sincere.

This was the Alex I knew, and I relaxed, pushing the warrior inside down, along with some of my guard.

I nodded and took a step back, distancing myself. "I need to get the headphones for you and the captain." I turned and headed upstairs.

Neither the cook nor the host was in the main cabin. I crossed to the sliders leading out to the deck. The two men were sharing a smoke, and neither were wearing the protective earphones.

The fact that they were laughing and talking and not displaying any hostility gave me an indication that perhaps I overreacted. I opened the slider and peeked out. "Excuse me, but can you tell me where I can find those earphones?"

The two stopped and glanced at me. Both tossed their cigarette butts in the water, and that's when I heard the soft crooning in the distance. That low melody that humans didn't recognize at first. I knew I was in trouble. I turned, trying to retreat as fast as I could, but Taavi, the cook, was faster.

He grabbed my arm and spun me towards him. I used the inertia of my spin to deliver a blow to his chest with the heel of my hand. His "oof" greeted my maneuver, and he went sailing back into Faraji. Both of them tumbled out onto the deck.

Out of the corner of my eye, I saw the earphones on the corner of the console and grabbed two pairs. I knew I should stay and take care of these two, but if I didn't get these on Alex and the captain, I'd be battling four men instead of just two.

I turned and ran smack into Alex's chest. He stared beyond me at the ocean night. I cursed under my breath.

His gaze lowered to mine. "Shit," he muttered and clamped his eyes and mouth shut. His entire body went rigid. His face scrunched in pain, and he forced his wrists in front of him, surrendering himself to me.

For the first time in my life, I witnessed what someone resisting the siren's call looked like, and it took me by surprise. I stared at him, dumbfounded, until the pitch of the song changed, growing louder and more insistent as Jeremiah got closer to the boat.

I knew my window of opportunity was mere seconds. I whispered a spell, and the small cuffs on my bracelet grew to normal size. With a twist of my wrist, I had the handcuffs open and was able to get one cuff tightened around Alex's wrist before weight slammed into me.

I flew past Alex onto the floor, yelping at the sudden pain in my hip. I may be quasi-immortal, but that didn't mean I didn't bleed or bruise. This one was going to take a bit of healing. If I didn't get this under control within the next few minutes, I might be put in a very compromising position.

I hopped to my feet before Faraji reached me and executed a foot sweep, knocking him down. Alex still stood in place, but his eyes were open and locked on the handcuff dangling from his wrist. Taavi wasn't far behind Faraji, and I took him down with a spin kick, knocking him out cold.

Alex's attention moved from the metal to me. His gaze turned into a glare. He lifted his cuffed hand and pointed to it. The move held more of an accusation than words would have.

I cursed under my breath because I might have to hurt him. Before I could take a step in his direction, arms wrapped around me like a vise, trapping my arms to my side. I threw my head back, but all I connected with was a chest. I kicked my legs back, struggling in his grip.

"Alex, help me," I said.

His face scrunched in pain. "Let her go." He took a step forward. His face smoothed out.

"Fuck you," Faraji growled close to my ear.

"She's mine," Alex said through clenched teeth, closing the distance. His fists clenched.

I shivered at the murderous glare. I wasn't sure whether the fire in his eyes was fueled by the siren song or just someone manhandling me.

My heel hit Faraji's shin just right, and he roared. His grip slipped, and I was able to scissor my arms wide and break his hold. My feet hit the ground, and I reached to my right, catching his shoulder and arm in my grip, and rolled him right over my hip. He landed between me and Alex. I took a step backwards, looking for some distance.

That was a dangerous move. I stumbled on Taavi and landed on my ass a few feet behind him.

Alex closed the distance and stopped, staring down at me, his expression transitioning between concern and anger. I rolled back and climbed to my feet, looking between him and Faraji, who now stood right behind Alex.

Taavi moaned from the floor. My skin flushed hot with panic. I met Alex's gaze, and the man I had fallen for was not there anymore. A feral monster had replaced him with one thing in its sights.

Me.

"I don't want to hurt you." I put my hands out, assessing the chances of getting Alex and Faraji neutralized before Taavi gained consciousness.

Alex's slow smile sent a shiver through me.

"Oh, but I want to hurt you." He stepped over Taavi. The darkness in his eyes reminded me of the devil.

I froze, but the jangle of his handcuffs pulled me out of my momentary paralysis. He pounced, and I moved, grabbing his reaching arm, and using his motion against him to slam him into the wall behind me.

I turned and ducked under Faraji's hook, coming up with my shot to the side of his face and knocking him off balance. That gave me enough time to thrust my knuckles into his temple. Faraji crumpled to the ground just as Alex tackled me.

We rolled across the floor, and he ended on top. He grabbed my arms and slammed me against the wood grain beneath me. His grip was tight enough to bite into my skin. A low growl came from deep in his throat.

"Damn it, Alex, you don't want to do this," I hissed up at him.

"Every time you tell me I don't want something, I see red," he snarled, but he didn't make any move beyond that first slam.

The groans from the other side of the room permeated my brain. I took a quick look at the two men slowly coming to.

"Baby, if you don't want to see me ravaged by those men, let me go. Let me take care of this." I used the softest, most seductive voice I could without engaging my song, praying it would reach my Alex.

He blinked and glanced toward Faraji and Taavi. His eyes flashed just as his face turned almost a purple red. He snarled and let go of me. I let him get to his feet before I swept him to the ground. I needed him safe, not in the middle of this battle.

"I'm sorry, baby," I whispered and slammed his temple.

At the very least, he would be disoriented long enough for me to get him somewhere where he couldn't hurt himself. I dragged him out on the deck, threaded his free arm around the outside railing, and snapped the cuffs closed.

I leaned over and placed a kiss on his forehead, then went inside to find those headsets before the others woke up. I grabbed a pair and went back outside to fit them over Alex's ears, praying that it might stop the degeneration of his mind.

I stepped inside, and the main floor was empty. Neither Faraji nor Taavi were anywhere in sight. My skin went cold. The siren song was loud enough to be close, and I couldn't hear any shuffling in the room over my brother's damn voice.

"Jeremiah, shut the fuck up!" I screamed.

The song stalled, and a nervous heat filled my bones. My brother was close enough to hear me scream. I slunk farther into the room, holding my breath as I inched past the helm, which was one of the few places someone could hide. By the time I got through the room, I knew they were no longer here, which meant they either disappeared to our quarters or the crew's quarters.

I turned back towards where I cuffed Alex and froze.

"Looking for these things?"

His voice hadn't changed in all these years. I stared into the neon-blue eyes of my brother. He held fistfuls of hair from each limp body in his grasp. Faraji and Taavi stared aimlessly toward the stars as their wet clothing dripped on the deck. Their blank expressions faced me, while their bodies faced the water. Jeremiah had snapped their necks, twisting them one hundred and eighty degrees. The faint stench of urine mingled with the sea air.

My heart slammed in my chest. Alex was still out there. I had to control my breathing, otherwise I would end up hyperventilating. Jeremiah might not know about him or the captain yet. Especially if they both were still unconscious, but the moment he sensed them, they were as good as dead.

My brother tossed each body to the side. They slapped the deck like wet fish, bringing a heinous smile to Jeremiah's face. His form held gray-green scaled legs that would return to a single powerful tail once he was submerged in the water. He stepped inside the cabin with a glare that clearly conveyed I was next.

"Jeremiah, please don't."

He stopped, staring at me through narrowed eyes. "How do you know my name?" His wet voice filled the room.

I forgot what we sounded like in our native form. The song differed from the voice. I had seen humans piss their pants at the sound of us talking. It had a terrifying, gravelly quality, as if we had a pint of sand in our cheeks while trying to talk around a gallon of water. It sounded like a walking corpse.

"I was the one who got you out of hell." I stood tall. I looked nothing like I had the last time I saw him. I had hidden him away before Fate got her grubby little hands on me.

A guttural growl gurgled in his throat. "She is dead."

"No, Jeremiah, I'm alive. It's me, Kylee." I opened my arms wide. "This is what Fate did to me."

He charged. "I killed her!" he shouted and swiped his clawed hand at me.

I jumped back, but not far enough. His nails dug bloody welts across my abdomen, shredding my shirt.

"I killed her a thousand times," he roared and swiped again.

This time I threw myself backwards over the edge of the couch, rolling over the cushion until I landed on my feet on the other side. Adrenaline burned through my veins as I set myself for the next attack.

"Stop this shit right now!" I commanded.

A muffled yell from downstairs pulled his attention from me. My heart dropped. The captain was an innocent, just like the crew members that my brother killed, and he didn't have a headset on.

I scrambled, trying to put myself between this evil version of my brother and the stairwell. Jeremiah's backhand hit, knocking me clear across the room. I slammed into the wall with such force, I swore my skull cracked.

Dazed, I tried to force my eyes to focus. The siren song mingled with the high-pitched whine in my head. My brother disappeared down the stairs. I used the wall to climb to my feet. Shaking my head just made the world tip worse.

A blurry duo stepped into the room. I covered my ears at the sharp knifing sounds, but even with them covered, I heard his command.

"Kill her." Jeremiah took a seat in one of the captain's chairs to watch the massacre.

The captain crossed the distance with his wrists free of the bonds I had left him in, but the rope stretched between his tightly clasped fists, taut with the pressure. His angry gaze dropped from my face to my shredded shirt and my bare legs. When his eyes traveled back up my body, he snapped the rope.

I tried to move, to turn and run away, but the rope caught me under the chin, yanking me back. The captain tightened it like a noose, cutting off my ability to breathe. I grabbed at it as he yanked harder, pressing his body against my back, pinning me to the wall.

The suggestive movement of his hips pulled a chuckle from my brother. I clawed at the rope, trying to get a little slack to draw a breath. The rope loosened for a second, long enough for my underwear to be ripped off. The captain's hands pressed against the wall on either side of my head, pulling the rope in opposite directions, closing down my trachea.

If I didn't act now, I would not survive. The captain rubbed himself against my backside, and just as he pulled away, readying himself to take me, I stomped my heel on the top of his foot with everything I had left.

It was enough to stun him, but his grip on the rope didn't let up. I tried to twist, but he body slammed me against the wall. My head hit the wood, and I saw stars. He tried to force my legs wide. I kicked my heel upwards. His thighs tightened on my ankle before I reached my goal. My strength was waning, and my lungs burned.

One of his hands dropped away from the wall, and the rope around my throat loosened. I jabbed my elbow back, connecting with a set of ribs. I followed with my other elbow. The captain grabbed my ankle and twisted, knocking me to the ground. I stared up at him holding my foot. His pants were crumpled around his ankles. I realized he no longer held the rope.

I kicked with my free leg, hitting home. His grip on my ankle released, and I rolled away, peeling the rope from my neck. I stood, using the upward movement to jab my palm into his nose. He went flying backwards onto the floor, his body jerking uncontrollably until he stilled. A small stream of yellow, pungent urine escaped.

I closed my eyes for a second. After the reality that I killed the captain settled, I turned a glare at my brother. "You bastard." My raw throat only produced a hiss.

He stood and crossed the room, cornering me. I had no more strength to fight him and no voice to defend myself. His sharp claws penetrated my shoulder, and I let out a squeak of protest.

If I died now, Alex would surely die. Just the flash of his face in my mind set my blood on fire. I yanked away from my brother just as the horn of another fishing vessel reached my ears.

Jeremiah's blades retracted. "I'll be back. Be a good girl and just sit down until I get back. You, I want to kill slowly. I want to sap your strength right from your bones." He smiled and disappeared out the front. A splash followed, along with the lull of his voice.

Chapter 10

WITH EVERY MUSCLE IN my body hurting, I crawled towards the deck, dragging the dead captain with me. Each movement came with the assault of one of my brother's memories. Somehow, when his nails penetrated my skin, I received some sort of nightmarish transmission. The devil sent our spawn one by one to drag Jeremiah back to hell, but my brother killed every one of my daughters.

The last one Lucifer sent was a dead ringer for me, right down to the sea-colored eyes. I recognized that child. She had been my first, but she was faithful to the devil, shunning me. She went after Jeremiah with a vengeance, but was not strong enough to resist his song, even with the devil's blood running through her. The little witch made my brother believe she was me. No wonder he wasn't buying my story.

I stopped at the control panel and pulled myself up, flipping the switch to lift the anchor. Then I continued towards the deck and the dead crew members. I used the remainder of my energy to push all three of them off the edge into the Mediterranean Sea.

I stumbled to Alex and checked his pulse as the drift of the sea took us south. He was still breathing. I said a small prayer to keep it that way. My head dropped into his lap as exhaustion, pain, and my brother's memories swirled in my head.

If Alex woke and killed me, so be it. At least I would be with him until the end. My eyes closed, and blackness sucked me under.

THE CLANG OF METAL against metal pulled me from slumber, and my eyes opened to the morning sky. Alex banged his wrists against the bar, his teeth bared in aggravation. I rolled away out of range and dragged myself up on the railing. My movement caught his attention, and his glare landed on me.

He blinked as his gaze traveled from my head to my toes, and then his eyes closed. A crease appeared between them for a moment.

"Did I..." His eyes opened, and his gaze met mine.

I shook my head. "No."

"I can't hear." Panic filled his voice.

I stepped close enough to pull the headphone away from his ear. "I covered your ears. I think we are far enough away to be out of range, but I'm going to leave them where I can cover your ear quickly if I need to, just in case." I recovered his ear and headed inside. I needed something to wash the sour taste from my mouth and I couldn't leave him standing out on the deck all day. I grabbed a chair for him to sit in and a bottle of water for both of us.

"Where is the captain?" he asked as he took a seat in the chair I offered.

Instead of answering, I offered him a sip of water, holding the bottle for him while he quenched his thirst. I moved the headphone away from his ear and took a seat a few feet away.

"Unfortunately, no one else survived, and I think the only reason I'm still breathing is another ship came into the area." I rubbed my sore face and stood to retreat inside. I needed some form of clothing instead of just a torn shirt. I slid on my bathing suit and cover-up because anything else would irritate the cuts across my stomach, and the light fabric would be perfect in the hot Mediterranean sunshine.

I rifled through Alex's bag and found what I deemed would be a comfortable pair of shorts. I would also have to figure out something in the way of a commode for him because he would not be un-cuffed until I figured out how to reverse the effects.

I knew of only one way to do that, but even after the heinous way Jeremiah treated me, I wasn't mentally or physically ready to run Neptune's trident through him. I needed a good meal and a little more rest before I took my brother on.

I stepped outside with Alex's shorts in my hand. "I figured you might like a pair of shorts instead of just your underwear."

He nodded. "I could use a shower."

"Not going to happen, hon." I placed the shorts on the arm of the chair and pulled the underwear he put on before our flight off him. I smiled up at him as I took the shorts in hand. "I could leave you commando, if you'd like."

He rolled his eyes. "I'd prefer not to get a sunburn on my dick. But before you put my shorts on..." He turned and leaned into the railings, relieving himself in the ocean. "Now you can help put those on," he added when he finished.

I pulled his shorts up to his thighs, and as I stood to finish dressing him, I realized my mistake. I had stood between his arms. He slammed me into the railing and smiled down at me.

The intensity in his eyes both thrilled me and sent a shiver of fear to my core. His mouth dipped as if he was going to kiss me, but the gentle graze of his lips slid under my jaw instead. His tongue skimmed my neck, and his teeth clamped down on my earlobe.

The sudden pain of teeth cutting into my flesh pulled a gasp from me.

"Let me out of these cuffs," he whispered through clenched teeth.

"I can't," I said, trying not to whine from the pain gripping my ear.

"I'll tear your throat out with my teeth if you don't."

His grip on my ear increased. I cried out. He pressed harder against me, trapping my hands between us. I let go of the edges of his shorts and grabbed his cock, applying enough pressure to convey that I meant business. The pressure on my ear let up, but he didn't let go.

"Alejandro, you are hurting me." I squeezed harder.

"That's the point, Kylee." His strained voice whispered in my ear.

I dug my nails in. Alex recoiled with a gasp, giving me a window. I slid out from under his arms and out of reach of his only true defense. He glared at me from over his shoulder, my blood dripping from his lips. I circled behind him and hiked up his shorts before collapsing in the chair a few feet away from him.

"You still want to kill me?" I asked.

He smiled with blood-smeared teeth. The crazy was back. I closed my eyes, burying my face in my hands. The only way to free him of this curse was to kill Jeremiah. I got up to go inside the cabin.

"You can't leave me here," he said.

I stopped with my back to him, debating what to say. I turned, crossed to him, and put the headphones back on. I didn't want him getting to where self-harm came into his mind. At least he was still in murder mode, which gave me a bit of hope. Once the disease advanced to the suicidal stage, there was no going back, even if the host who caused it was eliminated.

I left him cursing up a storm and went to find food. Maybe a decent meal would give both of us a small reprieve. I shuffled around the kitchen, finding eggs and bacon, and I whipped them up along with a few slices of toast. I brewed coffee, too.

With a fully loaded tray, I headed out to the deck, setting the food down on the table in the center. Instead of attending to Alex, I ate my fill and leaned back in the seat, sipping my coffee and assessing his mood. His gaze was glued to the plate piled with eggs and bacon.

"Are you going to behave?" I asked.

When he didn't respond, I nearly laughed at my stupidity. The man couldn't hear me, so I finally picked up the plate and a fork and stood. His gaze followed the plate until I stopped a foot away from him, and then he finally met my gaze and licked his lips.

I took a piece of bacon and fed it to him, leaving a large, last piece because I didn't want my fingers near his teeth. At least he still had some reasoning skills. For that, I was thankful. He ate every bite I gave him, and when the plate was empty, I set it on the table and grabbed the coffee I made for him.

I held the cup while he took a sip and closed his eyes. "You certainly know how to treat your prisoners," he said, opening his eyes again. The glare was there, but it was clouded by gratefulness.

I moved the earphone and said, "Yeah, well, I still care about you." I replaced it and brought the plates back to the kitchen to clean up the dishes.

The mundane activity seemed to clear my mind. I debated on staying inside or going out on the deck and subjecting myself to his heckling and glares. I needed rest, and I needed to figure out a plan, but I also didn't want to leave him alone. I grabbed a couple of waters and went back out into the sunshine.

I put one of the bottles in his hand and sat down with mine. He stared at the plastic and then at me. "What the hell am I supposed to do with this?"

"Figure it out," I said, mouthing the words as articulately as I could. It was his problem right now. I wasn't in a helping mood beyond feeding him. I turned and took the seat that looked out over the sea. No landmasses were visible from any direction. I sipped my water, letting the scenery calm me.

"You really were one of those things?"

I turned, meeting his stare. He had been out cold when my brother was on the boat. Or so I thought.

He chuckled a little. "I played dead. Especially after he snapped Taavi's neck."

I looked away. I didn't want to discuss this with his warped mind. Alex was a smart man, and he knew me well enough to play psychological games with me.

"Well, were you?"

I nodded without making eye contact.

"Will you turn into one of them again?"

Disgust laced his voice, and I cringed. I shook my head. The form I had now was forevermore, at least until I was delivered to the gates of hell. Then who knows what the devil would do?

"Are you going to look at me?" His voice echoed over the water.

I stood and marched over to where he stood, moving the earphone. "You were not even supposed to be on this trip!" I got right in his face, letting the anger of the situation surface. "You decided you just had to save my ass. Well, you did a bang-up job of that!"

He recoiled and blinked in a way that led me to believe I reached the true man and not this thing driven to violence by my brother.

"I nearly was gang raped because I was so concerned about you." My skin heated with the fury filling me. I pointed to the rope burns around my neck. "The captain thought it would be fun to choke me to death while he banged me." The emotions coiling inside wound up to where I was now yelling. "And my brother doesn't believe I am who I am because the devil kept sending my offspring to kill him. He never saw me in this form, and in his mind, he already killed me!"

The color leaked from his face.

"So any chance I had of talking him out of continuing this insane path he has taken is gone. I have to kill him in order to save your ass." I poked him in the chest and took a few steps back before I did anything more. "The only reason I'm not unlocking you and letting you finish me is what would come next."

He cocked his head, and his forehead creased.

"I'll spend the rest of eternity at the hands of Lucifer. I crossed him once by freeing my brother and escaping from hell. He's had millenniums to stew over that, and the time I spent at his mercy before will look like a fun trip to Disney Land in comparison." I took a deep breath. "If I fail, I end up at Lucifer's mercy. If I use my voice and an innocent dies, I end up in hell. If I free you, you will kill me, and at this point, I'm not sure I would stop you. If that happens, I end up being filleted for the rest of eternity."

Alex slowly sat down.

"May God have mercy on me, because when I take my brother's life, I know where he is going. I'm sentencing him to an eternity of anguish."

My vision blurred, and I swiped at my hot face, wiping tears I didn't realize I was shedding.

"Damn it, why did you have to get on that plane?" I collapsed in the chair, facing him.

Silence fell between us.

"You... you had children?"

I met his gaze. "Lucifer's favorite pastime was taking advantage of me and dropping me back in his fish tank until I birthed his hideous spawn. I had zero choice in the matter, so no. I did not have children. I had abominations."

Chapter 11

THE CALM OF THE sea lulled me. I stood on the bow at the farthest point from where Alex was chained. The soft crooning of Bruno Mars filled my head, but it still didn't take away the burn of Alex's silent disappointment. I couldn't deal with the disgust written on his pursed lips, as if I had given him a sour lemon instead of the facts. His judgment, along with Jeremiah's memories, raked at my nerves.

It was one thing to deny I ever had offspring when I had very few memories of them, but seeing each of their deaths through Jeremiah's eyes left me unable to cope. Each spawn that he killed took a piece of his sanity, turning him into the lunatic I saw last night.

I wondered if the same would be said of me after I slayed him.

The railing under my hands vibrated as if Alex was intentionally banging it. I tore my earphones off my head and turned towards the back of the boat.

"Kylee!" Alex's hoarse voice called.

I made my way aft, stepping onto the deck. His gaze was glued to something starboard, and I squinted into the sunlight, shielding my eyes with my hand. Light reflected off the hull of another boat coming in our direction. It was far enough away for the sound not to reach us yet, but I had a sinking feeling they weren't just heading on a lucky trajectory.

I tapped Alex on the shoulder and he jumped. His head swiveled toward me, and the tension filling his form eased a fraction. I stepped inside and took the helm, firing up the engines. I wasn't sure where to run, but I knew there was no other option.

It was probably a pirate craft, the Hellenic Coast Guard, or the boat that had saved my ass last night. Either way, an encounter would be no good. I couldn't explain Alex to a right-minded person, and I certainly couldn't let him loose, even if I was ordered to. If it was a pirate vessel, I wasn't sure what would happen.

I glanced starboard, and the single boat in the distance was now three. My heart dropped. There were no flashing lights, so my logical mind ruled out the Coast Guard. While it still could be Jeremiah's victims, I highly doubted they would be sane enough to launch a multiple craft attack.

Which left the only logical explanation. Pirates. After all, this was a hell of a boat, and it had just been drifting on the wind until a few minutes ago.

"Shit," I muttered and set course for the Egyptian coast.

With the autopilot set, I had to get Alex off the deck. Otherwise, he'd be killed instantly by whoever stepped on board. I muttered an incantation, and a key charm grew to a normal size. I unclasped it from my bracelet. With a few strides, I crossed to Alex, moving his earphone.

"If they board, we're both dead." I unhooked one cuff and stepped back.

He glanced at me and turned, heading inside. I followed a safe distance behind, and when he disappeared into the head, I went back to the helm. He came out a few minutes later and stopped a few paces away from me.

"Why don't you take a seat," I said, concentrating on pushing the engine as fast as the thing would allow. "And put those things back on," I added, nodding towards the earphones hanging around his neck.

He stepped behind me and grabbed my arms, slamming me forward over the console. His hands were already moving, pushing my swimsuit down enough for his fingers to access the warm recesses between my legs. My shoulder hit the engine kill switch. I tried to push him away. I could not have this distraction.

"Alex, we need to get the hell away from here," I said, but the urgency in my voice was lost in his purr as his fingers slid inside me.

His hand in the center of my back kept me facedown on the hard surface as his stroke became more of an assault.

"I need this," he whispered. His hips thrust forward, filling me with his length.

I cried out, but it was more from the surprise of his entry than pain or fear. His fingers manipulated my sensitive nub in slow circles. Whatever arguments I had were lost in the sensation of him rocking in and out of me in such slow strokes that I thought I would go insane.

The hand planted in the middle of my back slid to the base of my neck and snaked to the front of my throat. His grip tightened as his stroke increased. He pulled me to his chest, squeezing my windpipe hard enough to restrict my breathing, but not enough to close it down.

The sensation of him fucking me, along with the pressure on my neck, turned on an all-consuming fire that wiped my memory of danger. All I had was this moment, this pleasure laced with pain.

His hand moved from my throat, and he pulled my legs wide, lifting me until I kneeled on the edge of the helm. I pressed my hands against the edge of the backsplash, pushing into each of his thrusts. When he pulled away, I moaned, feeling empty without him, but then his cock breached my ass.

My moan shut off when his hand clamped around my throat again. His other hand resumed playing with my clit, creating a delicious heat through my body.

"Cum for me, baby," he whispered in my ear while his fingers still caressed me. His length slammed into me, pulling out a wheezing gasp. "I want you to drench the helm," he added, speeding up his movement.

He knew how to manipulate a woman's body with his hand. I had a moment to wonder what his mouth would be like before his teeth bit down on my shoulder, creating a new pain that blended with the bliss. I panted beneath his hold as he growled my name low in his throat.

My body tightened in anticipation of the buildup pooling in the center of my being. His grip tightened in response, cutting off my airway. My body didn't have the presence of mind to panic. Not at first, not when all my pleasure centers were pulsing with the need to release.

I bucked with the power of my orgasm, unable to draw air into my lungs, my body clenched with the strength of it. He pushed deep into me, crying out my name as he released with such force it caused another orgasm. This time, I did exactly as he had asked—I came so hard I sprayed the console.

His grip on my throat didn't release. In fact, he squeezed tighter as his body shuddered with aftershocks. I grabbed the cuff still clasped to his wrist and tried pulling. His lips found the nape of my neck, and he nibbled on the skin.

I yanked harder.

"Just go with it, Kylee," he whispered in that cold, empty voice.

The languid aftereffects of a soul-searing orgasm disappeared, replaced by the burn in my oxygen-starved lungs. He had me in a position that I could do little more than flail my arms. I tried pulling my legs together, but between the pressure on my throat and his hand still continuing to play me like a human guitar, I couldn't find the strength to move my body in a way to break his grip.

White spots filled my vision. I scratched at the hand around my throat. I bucked and one of my legs came out from under me. I used it to push off the console, sending the two of us onto the floor. The impact made his grip slip, and I twisted, rolling away from him as fast as I could. I coughed, gasping for air as the spots covering my vision faded. I pulled my bikini bottoms back in place and climbed to my feet.

He lay on his back, staring at the ceiling, his chest rising and falling with his exertion. A tear spilled from the edge of his eye as he slowly turned his gaze to mine.

"I don't want to kill you. I really don't. But I have to." He sat up.

My chest hurt from more than oxygen starvation. Murder reflected in his eyes. I executed a roundhouse kick, connecting with his head, praying it wouldn't kill him.

He went down hard. I paused a minute before I crossed to check if he was still alive. My fingers searched for a pulse, and when I found one, I let out a shaky breath. My throat closed on the sob building there. Somewhere, some angel was looking after this man.

I was sure I'd have a lot of explaining to do when he finally snapped out of the siren's spell, but for now, the bruise on his temple had already grown into a knot that would likely hurt for weeks, much like my nearly crushed windpipe.

The roar of the engines gave me a start. I glanced out the window, judging distances. I had a choice. Safeguard Alex or try to outrun the fleet of three boats closing in. I glanced down at my unconscious ward and made my decision.

I dragged Alex into the bathroom, looking around to make sure nothing he could hurt himself with was within reach. I sat him on the commode and cuffed him to the plumbing. He would be uncomfortable, but he would also be alive.

Once the headphones were secure, I wrapped gauze that I found in the first aid kit under the sink around his head, including his eyes to make sure the headset stayed in place no matter what. He would be disoriented as hell, but I didn't care. At least he would be safe and had an added bonus of being perched on the loo.

I exited and closed the bathroom door just as the boats flanked the yacht. I ran my hand through my hair and glanced at the soiled helm. There was nothing I could do about cleaning it at the moment.

The unmistakable smell of sex filled my nostrils, and I prayed those who were boarding wouldn't catch it on the air, especially if they were siren influenced. There were too many of them for me to fight back. My heart banged in my chest. I had a split second to figure out a plan.

I collapsed on the floor within sight of the door, saying a brief prayer that this was the right course of action. If I was wrong, there could be dire consequences, and I would have to tap into my siren voice to save Alex's ass.

Chapter 12

FOOTSTEPS OF AT LEAST three people shuffled onto the deck. I made the muscles in my body relax. I hoped I would look like an unconscious woman to whoever boarded our vessel.

It took me a few moments to nail down the language they spoke. Arabic. My mastery of languages helped, but for some reason, the dialect they were using was foreign to me. I only could pick out one of every few words. Something poked me, and I allowed a small moan to come from my lips. I fluttered my eyelids open but let them close again after getting my first view of seven men with machine guns.

A slap stung my cheek, and I resisted the punch that almost got away from me. Instead, I blinked my eyes open and slowly glanced around, letting my eyes widen. I tried to scooch away from the men like any sane woman would do if they were woken to a room full of men with guns.

One of them grabbed my hair, showing it to the others, telling them I would bring a lot of money on the black market. The other argued I was damaged goods. The one with my hair crouched next to me.

"Where are the men who did this to you?" he asked in perfect French.

I just stared at him. He tried again in Italian and then finally tried English.

I let my chin quiver and shrugged. "I hurt him and he stumbled that way." I pointed towards the deck. The only other area accessible from off the deck was the crew quarters.

The fool looked up and pointed the group towards the deck, leaving only the two of us in the cabin. His grip on my hair loosened, but it didn't release.

"How did you hurt him?" he asked, using a calm voice, but he was clearly assessing me.

"I kneed him in the balls," I said. "And the last thing I remember is him stumbling out there, and then I blacked out."

The gun was slung over his shoulder behind him, and the others were out of eyesight. I shot the heel of my palm up, catching him under the chin with all the aggravation mixing in my blood. The audible snap of the jackass's neck sounded through the room.

I dragged him behind the helm and yanked the gun off his shoulder. After checking both the clip and the safety, I set the gun to controlled live fire. Positioning myself behind the kitchen counter where I could see both the deck and the front of the boat in the mirror above me, I leaned back and went over my options. I was too far away from the bathroom where Alex was bound to protect him from any stray bullets.

I was tempted to use my voice, but the ramifications if any of them got loose would be catastrophic, so I hunkered down and waited. If they all didn't come up at the same time, or if they came from opposite directions, I'd have to do something drastic. But until this played out, I wasn't going to get my panties in a bunch.

A radio squawked, and I jumped, but luckily my trigger finger didn't squeeze. I glanced around at the man I just killed and cursed under my breath. Shuffling noises below stopped, and then the fast patter of feet in both directions reached my ears.

Damn it all to hell. The element of surprise was gone, and now they would run in here with guns raised, if not already blazing. I took a deep breath and closed my eyes. The wisdom of this wasn't even on the map, but I couldn't let them shoot up the place.

I opened my mouth, willing the siren inside me to come forth. The first note was soft, almost soothing. The pounding feet slowed to a stop for a few beats before resuming at a slow pace. They arrived from both directions at the same time, their guns pointing at the ground now that I had them in my spell.

I altered a couple of notes and then stopped, waiting and watching the men in the mirror. The expressions changed on almost all the pirates, confusion turning to rage and guns raised, pointing at one another. I ducked farther down and covered my head the moment the bullets started flying. My ears rang with the discharge of so many weapons in the enclosed space. When the last body fell and silence blanketed the room, I stood from my hiding place.

Just to be sure, I squeezed the trigger, burying a bullet in each head before I ran to the deck where the boats were moored. I sprayed almost the full clip into two of the three hulls. I swung to the third one and faced the only person manning the boats. He pulled a sword and went to hop onto my deck.

The last of my bullets nearly cut the man in half. He fell back into the only viable boat. The others were already taking on water. I untied the sinking vessels and went inside to gather the dead. It took me a while to get them all in the boat where my sword-wielding foe had made a valiant, but vain attempt.

Untying the last skiff, I pushed it away from the yacht, emptied the rest of the bullets into the boat, and dropped each spent weapon in the sea, waiting until the boats had nearly submerged before I headed back inside. I stopped dead in the doorway, my eyes nearly bulging out of my head at the sight of a live pirate.

His gun was trained on the middle of my abdomen, and he smiled. None of the bullets had hit him. I never saw where he had hidden. In my haste to get these shits off my boat, I hadn't done a head count.

"Hands up," he said, but his voice wasn't clear. It was nasally and slurred like that of a person who had no mastery over his tongue.

The truth hit like a boxer's jab. This pirate was deaf.

I obeyed, putting my hands in the air. The fact that he was deaf saved his life, but now I was at his mercy. By the glare he leveled at me, I didn't think he was capable of compassion.

He pointed the gun to the spot in front of him. I slowly crossed, wondering if there was a chance to get out of this. I stalled a few feet away. His face scrunched in fury, and he tapped the floor right in front of him.

I took another step. My mouth went dry.

"Right here!" he bellowed and pulled the trigger, sending a round into the floor.

I stepped to the spot he shot. His backhand spun me onto my knees.

"What happened?" he barked and grabbed my cheeks, forcing me to look at him.

"I... I shot them." I knew lying wasn't an option.

"No. Before. Downstairs, we ran and stopped. Then they all went crazy killing each other!"

I shrugged, my mind spinning to come up with a creative answer that would freak him out enough for me to get the gun out of his hands. "I don't know. I heard someone singing and then all hell broke loose. That's exactly what happened before the captain of this boat tried to kill me." I pointed to the bruises on my neck, praying this asshat knew enough about sea lore to make him nervous.

The anger thinning his lips turned into wide-eyed fear. His gaze darted around the boat. I went to stand, and the barrel swung back in my direction. His eyes narrowed as he studied me.

"Take off shirt," he commanded.

With shaking hands, I peeled off my cover-up, revealing my skimpy bathing suit, along with the scrapes and cuts of the last few days, some of which still oozed.

He grabbed a handful of my hair and pointed the barrel against my cheek. "I sell you."

I laughed, but he jammed the gun between my teeth. I gagged on the oily barrel, trying to recoil. I had no power over this crazy, deaf fuck.

"You my slave," he snarled. "You obey or die."

As if to make his point, he jammed the barrel of his gun farther down my throat. He pushed me back and pointed to the helm, handing me a slip of paper with coordinates.

I started the engine and plugged the coordinates into the computer, glancing at the location. He had me going to a port in Libya. I couldn't bring Alex back to land. Not with the sickness in him. I changed the direction, taking us opposite what I had plugged in, into the heart of the Mediterranean.

My only hope was to find my brother.

Deaf boy jabbed the gun into my lower back, hard. I turned, and he pointed to the ground in front of him. This time, an evil smile spread over his lips.

"Kneel and suck me, slave."

Jesus, I just stepped into the wrong pile of shit. I sank to the floor, and the barrel kissed my temple. A muffled cry came from the bathroom, but the deaf man with the gun didn't register Alex's angry rant the way I did. It was as if the action of this bastard brought my boyfriend out of the blackness I knocked him into.

I blinked at the mental reference. Boyfriend. What an odd thought to have right before I choked down another man's cock. The pirate tapped my temple. I glared up at him with my lips pressed together.

Instead of issuing another threat, the deaf asshole grabbed my elbow and jammed the gun into the center of my hand. The roar of the discharge filled the space. Pain locked down my ability to breathe. Then my exhale came in the form of a scream. I pulled my shattered hand to my chest as tears blinded me. Alex's rant changed from threats to my life to threats to whoever was harming his woman.

"Suck," the deaf fuck commanded, tapping my temple again.

My mouth was still open with pants of pain. He didn't care that I might bleed to death while giving him a blow job. All he cared about was his slave obeying. I had been in that position once before. I froze at the demon smile on this bastard. It reminded me too much of Lucifer.

My chest seized, and air wheezed in and out of my lungs. He reached for my arm again. This time, he might blow my hand clean off. I raised my good hand to the front of his cargo shorts and fumbled with the belt. I had sucked enough cock in my lifetime, but this was different. I had never been forced to give head. If I didn't find my brother, this would be my future until whatever benefactor bought me tired of my wiles and killed me. This was my penance for using my voice against humans and failing to bring my brother down the first time.

I unzipped the man's pants to the sound of Alex kicking the doors, stomping on the floor and screaming as if it had been his hand that had been shot to hell.

Deaf fuck pushed me away, cocking his head. He caught the vibrations of Alex's freak out. Hell, even I felt them through the floor, since any bounce of the hull shot waves of agony from my hand through the rest of my body.

I reached for the trident on my bracelet as deaf boy moved the gun toward the bathroom. The incantation fell from my lips. *"Deaus Neptunus in mari nascuntur tridentem istum mihi.*" Before the bastard knew what happened, the weapon grew and impaled him, slicing right through his body with a searing sizzle. The gun went off. He emptied the clip as he fell, shattering the sliders and drawing a bullet line through the ceiling. The gun lasted longer than he did.

I recounted the shrinking spell, "*Neptunus maris deus, fac mihi cessuros trident.*" The trident retracted back into the charm size in the palm of my hand. I clasped the bloody charm back onto my bracelet and headed to find the first aid kit. My hand needed attention before I could address another dead body.

Chapter 13

I SEARCHED EVERY ROOM on the boat except the bathroom where Alex was chained looking for another damn first aid kit and came up empty. I stopped in front of the bathroom and took a deep breath. When I threw the door open, his flailing and carrying on abruptly ceased. His entire body stiffened when my fingers grazed the front of his face. I pulled down the strip covering his eyes, leaving a bloody streak on the gauze.

"What the hell happened out there?" he asked.

It took me a minute to realize the red on the side of his head wasn't from my hand. I nearly ripped the gauze off his head in one sweeping motion. He winced as I pulled the headphones off. I stared at the welt cutting through his ear and followed the trajectory to the wall behind his head. A hole the size of a bullet met my gaze.

I sat down hard on the floor. A stray bullet from the shootout had torn through the gauze and must have knocked the headphones off enough for him to hear part of what happened. My good hand covered my mouth as I met his glare.

"What happened?" he snarled.

I found my wits and stood, putting some distance between us while I addressed my mangled hand with water from the sink.

"I used my voice and made them shoot each other. Unfortunately, there was a deaf one with them who lived." I clenched my teeth against the burn of clean water and glanced at Alex. "Your kicking and carrying on saved me."

He gave a huff and nodded towards my hand. "It certainly doesn't look like I saved you."

I bit my lip and slowly wrapped my hand in gauze. What I really needed was the ocean water and its healing properties. Instead, I poured some hydrogen peroxide on a towel and dabbed the cut along Alex's head and part of his cheekbone.

He winced away from my touch.

"Sit still."

"What are you doing?"

"I'm cleaning your gunshot wound." I stopped and glanced at him. "We both got lucky today. You've just got a flesh wound."

If the bullet had been even a half an inch to the left, he would have died. My hands shook as I cleaned the wound. The blood had already clotted, but he would have a visible scar on his cheek for a while.

I stepped back and leaned against the door. "I tried to secure the headphones with the gauze. That's why you couldn't see, and as much as I know you don't want me to do that again, I have to."

He went to argue, but I splayed my fingers at him, stopping whatever rant he was about to launch.

"I can't deal with you right now. I need to take care of the hole in my hand first." I turned and went to the helm to shut the engine off. I needed the ocean. I needed the warm waters of the Mediterranean. I needed the magic of home.

I dropped anchor and went to the bow of the boat. The deck was a god-awful mess. I knew I'd have to climb up that way, but for now, I needed a clean view of the sea, not one marred with death.

I dove off the bow, bracing myself for the pain of the water hitting my hand. It did not disappoint, and I gasped, nearly sucking in a lungful of water. I surfaced, coughing and sputtering. Forcing the water I inhaled out of my throat kept my mind off the debilitating agony gripping my hand. I slowly moved towards the stern, taking small strokes to stay afloat.

By the time I reached the back of the boat, the pain eased to a dull throb. I reached for the rail and held on for a moment, bringing my injured hand into view. The bones had already been reconstructed, and the skin was just beginning to thatch back together. I squashed the urge to itch it and dunked it back under the surface.

This was one of the curses of my existence. The ocean had always healed what ailed me. Cuts, bruises, and breaks all disappeared after a dip in the sea. It revitalized me, but there were limitations. I was sure death was one of them, but I was never dumb enough to play out that curiosity.

I glanced down at the only other limitation that I was aware of. The only wounds that hadn't healed were those delivered by another siren.

Cuts still traversed my stomach, and the wound in my shoulder still oozed. My stomach held red welts, but that shoulder wound needed addressing.

I climbed out of the water, taking as much care as possible to avoid the blood streaks on the deck, but it was nearly impossible. When I stepped back into the bathroom, Alex's eyes widened.

I glanced in the mirror at my unmarred neck. The bruises on my face were gone as well, and my hand, while itching to high heaven, didn't show any signs of a bullet shattering it.

"You never wondered why I used to go swimming at odd hours of the night?" I picked up the bottle of hydrogen peroxide and dumped a healthy amount into the wound on my shoulder. It bubbled and continued to ooze as I searched the cabinets for something more convenient than a strip of gauze and bigger than a Band-Aid.

"Why didn't that heal?" he asked, nodding towards my shoulder.

"Because it's from another siren." I didn't go farther into the lore with him. Instead, I found a larger bandage and pressed it over the wound.

"So... if you died, all I would have to do is dump your body in the ocean and you'd come back to life?"

I rolled my eyes at him and turned to leave.

"I'm asking a serious question."

"The dead don't rise." I stared at him for a moment, and that hopeful glint in his eyes faded. "I need to find another pair of earphones for you."

"Why?"

I stopped in the doorway and hung my head before I glanced back at him. "My voice is the only thing that will get me close enough to my brother to use this." I flicked the trident charm on my bracelet.

"I'm already doomed," he said. "I'd really like to hear your voice in my head."

"Killing my brother will break the spell on you."

His eyebrow rose.

"And anyone else still afflicted with the siren sickness."

I left him to noodle on that while I started the tedious work of cleaning the cabin, including getting rid of the last body. There was only so much I could do, even with the strong cleaners I found in the staff quarters. I had no idea how long I scrubbed, but I couldn't get it all clean. There was too much blood on the fabric. Luckily,

I was able to get the floors clean, and at least Alex had been quiet while I cleaned the cabin and deck. I had left the bathroom door open so he wouldn't feel so isolated.

When I finished, I grabbed the headphones along with earbuds that had been downstairs in the captain's quarters. He had an iPod in the charging station, and I plucked it from the base before heading back to Alex. He glared at me when I stepped into the room. "There's no chance you'll let me out of here, is there?"

"Afraid not."

He lashed out with his foot, and I caught it with my free hand before it connected.

"Do I need to tie your legs up too?"

The angry grimace transitioned into a playful smile. "Is that what you'd like to do?"

"Not particularly," I answered and slid to the side of the toilet where his legs couldn't reach. "I would really like *my* Alex back, because I think I might have fallen in love with him during the flight over here."

He blinked up at me and didn't fight as I fit the ear buds in and then placed the headphones over his ears. I chanced a quick peck on his lips before setting the iPod to shuffle and hitting play. I stepped away.

"I think I've been in love with you for a couple of years now," he whispered.

I paused in the doorway and met his gaze. For a moment, a shadow passed over his eyes like I wasn't supposed to hear what he'd just said. I gave him a nod and made my way to the newly cleaned helm. I lifted anchor and turned over the engine, letting it idle while I checked the historical coordinates.

The nice thing about this vessel was it had a log of wherever the boat engaged the anchor. I set course for the first anchor of our journey.

Chapter 14

THERE REALLY IS NO easy way to prepare yourself for killing someone. Let alone someone you love. No matter how many times I rolled it over in my head, I still came back to the option of talking sense into him. Logically, it sounded like a valid plan, but I knew better. Even if I looked like I had the day we escaped from hell, I'd still have a hard time convincing him of who I was.

"Damn it," I muttered, shaking the thought out of my head.

If one lived, the other died. My gaze traveled to the bathroom as the twilight created long shadows across the cabin. Alex had broken out in song a few times when something familiar came across the tunes I had on continuous shuffle. He was as tone-deaf as they came, and it was so endearing that tears sprang to my eyes.

The navigator beeped, and I glanced at the coordinates. This was where we were anchored the last time my brother struck. I shut the boat down, dropping the anchor.

Waiting was never my strong suit. Alex's intermittent singing pulled my attention away from detecting the siren song enough times for me to become truly annoyed.

I stood, and that was when I felt the tilt of the boat. The stern dipped, and I moved so I could see the deck.

Jeremiah climbed the step, his legs still forming, so his steps weren't steady yet. I glanced towards the bathroom. Alex had gone unusually quiet. Maybe he felt the disturbance, too.

My brother let out a soft scale of notes, as if he were testing the ship. I unclipped the trident and held it in my fist. The tongs singed my skin, but I ignored the discomfort, holding tighter instead.

When he stepped through what used to be the doorway, his eyes narrowed in my direction.

"You really shouldn't have used your voice again, Jeremiah," I said, my voice full of sadness.

He paused. I couldn't bring myself to utter the incantation that would bring the trident to full form. The resistance to killing my little brother kicked in. This was the boy I used to rock to sleep in my arms after our mother abandoned us. This was the kid I used to play hide-and-seek with in the coral reefs. This was my brother.

He hissed at me in such a way that I took a step back. "Why aren't you affected by my song?" he growled.

"Because I once swam in this sea and sang alongside you, luring humans to their death. Then the angels came and sentenced us to an eternity in hell."

He bellowed with rage and charged. I stood my ground, pivoting at the last moment. He sailed past me and slid to a stop, spinning back in my direction to launch at me. This time, I wasn't fast enough. His backhand caught my cheek, sending me falling to the side. I used the inertia to roll back on my feet.

Anger welled up inside me, exploding to the surface as a roar. "Why? Why did you break our pact?"

"The only pact I ever made was with my sister, and she is dead!" He moved towards me.

I tried to dodge to the side, but he still caught me, slicing across the same shoulder he injured before. I screamed and spun out of a direct hit. The look in his eyes was far beyond reason. He was going to tear me apart piece by piece if he had his way. Even knowing this didn't bring forth my self-preservation. I couldn't kill him to save my soul.

He closed the distance and shoved with his palms. I flew into the wall next to the bathroom entrance. The impact dazed me, but not enough for me to lose my grip on the trident. I glanced to my right and met Alex's wide-eyed stare.

The next moment, Jeremiah had his hand wrapped around my neck. He lifted me off my feet, slamming me back into the wall.

"No!" Alex yelled.

Jeremiah's attention jerked to the bathroom and the clear view of Alex tied to the toilet. "What have we here?"

His grip constricted my voice so I couldn't say the incantation to make the trident big. I couldn't defend myself, either. Struggling in his grip, I kicked out, but my human form was no match for Jeremiah. He was going to kill me in front of Alex.

"Hoc maior gratia!" Alex cried from the bathroom, using the same words I used to make the mace grow in my living room.

My right wrist grew heavy, and I realized just what Alex had done. I twisted my hand and gripped the handle of the mace, bringing the spiked ball straight up between my brother's legs.

His breath came out in an 'oof,' and then his grip on my throat disappeared as both his hands grabbed his private parts. I swung the mace like a bat while I had a moment of reprieve. It connected with his temple, knocking him to the ground. My bracelet snapped when I dropped the mace. I gave Alex a quick nod of thanks before moving out of Jeremiah's reach.

His glare lifted to me as blood dripped from the side of his face. The damage the supernatural tools I wielded were always significant no matter the creature. It was as if the weapons were charmed in some fashion, and it was no different against Jeremiah. I could hurt him with any number of weapons, but only one would kill him.

He let out a growl as he climbed to his feet. Instead of coming after me like I assumed, he turned towards Alex like a predator cornering his prey.

Hot venom filled my veins, and my protective instincts flared. My voice rose from the depths of my soul, singing a lullaby that I used to sing to Jeremiah when he was little.

His head whipped in my direction, and jaw dropped. He stopped dead in his tracks, turning towards me. I continued singing, and every fiber of my being screamed at the injustice of this moment. My skin burned with it, along with an ache in my chest that would overwhelm me if I let it.

He stepped towards me like he was in a dream, lulled by my song. My voice hitched. He swam in my vision and I blinked. Hot paths traced my cheeks. They did not stop, even as the song smoothed out in my throat.

Between verses, I whispered Neptune's incantation. *"Deaus Neptunus in mari nascuntur tridentem istum mihi."* And the trident grew to full height.

Jeremiah's gaze moved from me to the weapon I now held, and his eyes widened. I let the last verse roll from my lips, pulling his attention back to my tear-stained face.

"I'm sorry," I whispered and jabbed the business end of the trident towards his chest.

He parried, but not fast enough to miss the sting of the trident tearing through his arm. He bellowed his anger and grabbed for the staff. I twisted away, cutting his chest with the sharp point on the end opposite the trident fork.

His claws scraped my back, tearing the flesh as I spun. I stumbled back and caught myself before I fell. I aimed the forks at my bother as we circled.

"Kylee!" Alex's voice barreled from the bathroom.

I didn't pay any mind to Alex. I couldn't. Not right now. I was too engaged in this battle to let my attention wane. If Jeremiah got hold of the trident, I was dead.

"You share the same name as my dead sister." His gaze sharpened now that he was no longer under my siren spell. He jerked towards me.

I flinched, jabbing the weapon. He sidestepped and grabbed one of the trident forks, yanking me off balance with a bellow as the gold burned his skin. The trident slipped from my grasp, and I hit the floor flat out. The trident clattered a few feet away. I scrambled to my feet, diving for it.

The kick in my side sent me flying into the cabinets on the far side of the room. The shock of it left me disoriented until I drew a breath. Air seemed to revive the wild beast, twisting my bones inside me. I moaned at the pain searing my left side. I tried to get to my hands and knees, but I couldn't quite manage it.

My eyes focused on seeing Jeremiah step into the bathroom, out of sight.

"No," I whispered, but even speaking was painful.

Metal scraped against metal and Alex howled. I forced myself to my hands and knees just as Alex came flying out of the bathroom. He landed on his ass on the floor without headphones, and the cuffs were no longer on his wrists. The impact knocked an ear bud out of his ear.

He scrambled to his feet as Jeremiah stepped in the doorway and pointed towards the discarded trident.

"Kill her," Jeremiah ordered and sang the haunting tune of our ancestors. The one that incited murder in our victims.

Alex's body tensed, every muscle vibrating with the curse. He stepped towards the trident as if he wore lead shoes. His singular focus was on the weapon, and there was nothing I could do to stop him. If I engaged my voice, Alex would be doomed.

"You bastard," I whispered, glaring at Jeremiah as I pulled myself to my feet.

He stopped singing, turning his attention to me. "Come on, big sis. Let's hear that voice of yours. Let's see what you can do?"

Alex picked up the trident and stared at the tongs and the diamond embedded just above the staff. He twirled it and inspected the sharp point before turning his gaze to mine.

The darkness that lived in his eyes pulled a shiver from me. My Alex was no longer; he was my brother's puppet now. His movements were smoother as he turned and pointed the deadly dagger at me.

I couldn't bring myself to stop him, no matter how much my brother cajoled. Alex stopped in front of me, holding the trident out in front of him as if he was handling a bo staff in a martial arts class.

Jeremiah stepped behind him and tilted Alex's hand so the point was in line with my heart. He stepped back and smiled over Alex's head.

"Kill her," he said again, this time in a melodic whisper. One Alex couldn't ignore.

I met Alex's fogged gaze. "I love you, Alex."

The mist cleared for a fraction of a second. Just enough for my Alex to make an appearance. He jammed the trident backwards, spinning and lunging at the same time. The forks bit through Jeremiah's stomach. He let go of the staff as Jeremiah screamed in agony.

My brother's face transformed into a mask of fury, and he lurched forward, impaling Alex through the right side of his chest. Alex's cry mixed with my brother's growling roar as he continued towards me.

I grabbed the tip and muttered the incantation before Jeremiah could impale me. *"Neptunus maris deus, fac mihi cessuros trident."*

Alex bellowed his pain and collapsed as the trident staff shrunk.

The minute he hit the floor, I said the magic words again. *"Deus Neptunus in mari nascuntur tridentem istum mihi."*

The trident shot forth like a lightning bolt, but this time, the aim was true. The middle fork pierced right through my brother's heart. My chest ached and my throat tightened against the sudden swell of tears blinding me.

Jeremiah's eyes widened, and he looked down at the tongs embedded in his chest before his gaze returned to mine. "Kylee?" he whispered and then slowly sank to his knees. He transformed into his native merman form.

"I'm sorry, Jeremiah," I whispered and pushed harder until the bottom of the trident forks burned into his chest.

His tail banged the floor a couple times, and I waited until his last breath wheezed out of his lungs before I commanded the weapon to shrink back to trinket size. His body crusted over like an ancient sea coral that had been exposed for too long, freezing him forever in death.

My gaze moved to the trinket in my palm just before my knees gave way. I dropped to the floor and crawled to Alex. His breath was labored. I rolled him on his back, his pained gaze meeting mine.

"Kylee," he whispered and coughed blood.

I reached for my charm bracelet and found my wrist empty. I frantically scanned the boat cabin. I scrambled to my feet and stumbled across the room to where the bracelet lay still attached to the mace. My shrinking incantation sounded slurred, like I had a little too much wine, but I guessed that was from the bang on my head. I connected the trident charm and filtered through the rest of them until I came upon a delicate decanter. I twisted it off and crawled back to Alex, sputtering the right spell to make the ambrosia vial expand.

Thankfully, Alex was still breathing and conscious. I poured three drops in his mouth and peeled his shirt up to reveal the hole where the spike had gone through. I poured five drops of the ambrosia on his skin surrounding the injury.

"I'm sorry, sweetie. This is going to hurt." I rolled him over. He just groaned. This time, I poured what equaled a quarter cup of liquid right into the puncture and then turned him on his side.

He gasped as I held him in place. I capped the decanter, whispered the spell to shrink it back to charm size, and clasped it on my bracelet.

"I know it hurts," I said, as his jaw tightened. "But it will heal you."

"What is it?" he asked through labored breaths.

"Nectar of the Gods."

His eyebrows rose. "Immortality?"

I guessed he knew Greek mythology. Chuckling, I shook my head. "While it has healing qualities for humans like the ocean does for me, it does not make you immortal." I stoked his cheek gently. "Although one could argue that it can help you cheat death a time or two."

He laughed, but his laugh turned into a convulsing cough that sprayed blood everywhere. A wad of blood came up. Then he settled down with a groan, leaning into me. His breathing was less labored now, less like a wet rag than before. I lifted the shirt in the back and smiled at the entry wound. Instead of being an inch in diameter, it had shrunk to the size of a bullet in the short time we sat here. In no time, his skin would be smooth and unmarred.

I closed my eyes, and the world swam.

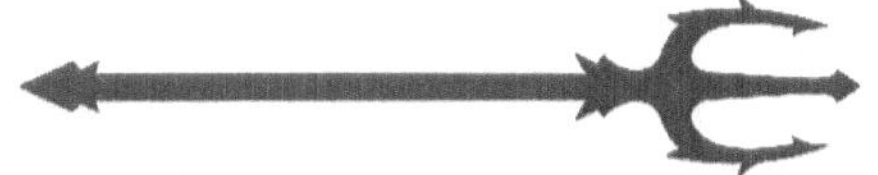

"KYLEE?"

A wet hand caressed my cheek. Weightlessness gripped me, yet my entire body felt heavy. It was an odd sensation.

"Kylee, please wake up."

The words whispered at a distance, but they pulled at me, drawing me closer.

"Please, please, wake up."

Lips drifted across mine. The softness was welcomed and sweet, and his breath tickled my face. Splashing taps on my cheek made me turn away.

"Kylee?"

My name hung on the air, and I blinked my eyes open. Alex's concerned gaze met mine. I lifted my head and winced. My muscles didn't like me very much, and I couldn't quite figure out where I was.

"Where are we?"

"We are in the emergency float on the deck. I filled it with sea water, so it's kind of like a kiddy pool." He wiped my cheek with water and helped me sit up. "It's not exactly clean, but I think it did the trick."

"What happened?"

"You passed out."

I had to suppress a 'duh.' The last thing I remembered was his wound healing, and then everything went black. I waited for more of an explanation.

"I think you might have crushed your entire ribcage and possibly shattered your shoulder. The back of your head was bleeding. I'm sure you have a hell of a concussion, and I think you may even have cracked your cranium. I have no idea how you did what you did at the end." He stopped and wiped his face. "Luckily, I remembered what the ocean did for you before. So..." He waved at the pool and gave me a shrug. "I didn't know if it would work, and I didn't have any magic elixir like you did."

My back stung to high heaven, but at least breathing didn't hurt like it had before. The water healed some of my ailments, but not the cuts from my brother's claws. I did a slow assessment of all my limbs, torso, and head. I seemed to be in one piece, even though my head still felt fuzzy.

"Kylee?" he asked after a few minutes of silence.

I turned to look at him.

"I remember... everything." His gaze dropped away from mine and he stood, retreating into the cabin now that he knew I was okay.

I climbed to my feet and stepped out of the makeshift tub. Glancing at the red-tinged water produced an unpleasant shiver. I had to have been bleeding pretty badly to turn an entire lifeboat full of sea water red. Either that or someone put food coloring in it as a poor joke.

Each step pulled at the cuts on my back. I winced as I walked carefully into the cabin. Alex was sitting on the couch, dripping bloody water all over the place. I almost said something, but a quick glance around quieted me. All the furniture in the room was splattered with blood, and the floor had a thick puddle where Alex had fallen. The crusted shape of my brother still sat in the same place as well.

The entire scene looked like it was cut right out of a B-horror flick.

"Are you okay?" I asked as I approached him.

Alex shook his head. "I tried to kill you more than once and I..." He waved towards the helm. A blush bloomed in his cheeks, spreading to his entire face. "I don't really know what that was." He avoided my gaze.

"You are a very strong man."

He covered his face with his hands.

"Look at me, Alex," I whispered as I took the seat opposite him. It was a struggle, but he finally met my gaze. "You resisted my brother's siren call more than once. That is something I have never seen before."

"I tried to kill you."

"Yeah, well, that roundhouse kick I did could have killed you, too. And my brilliant idea of making those pirates shoot each other nearly got you shot. A half inch the other way, and you would have died."

"I deserved it." His lips pressed together, and his brow creased in that familiar look of self-loathing.

I used to see that expression on his face any time he got into an argument with his ex-wife. "Don't do that."

"Do what?" His sharp gaze jumped to mine.

"Blame yourself."

He bit his lip and stared at me. "Kylee, I was still in there."

"I know. I'm still breathing."

His eyebrow went up.

"You have no idea how much willpower it takes to refuse to follow a siren's orders. My brother gave you a direct order to kill me. You didn't. Instead, you attacked him. That doesn't happen. Ever. I have seen husbands kill their wives and mothers slaughter their children without a blink. I've seen brothers and sisters turn on each other." I stopped and closed my eyes. "You are the only man that ever resisted. Why?"

He laughed. "Are you seriously asking that?"

I nodded.

He leaned forward. "I jumped on a plane and traveled halfway around the world to make sure you were safe. However misguided that was, that is not done simply out of friendship." He looked down at his hands clasped between his knees. "Did you mean what you said to me?" His gaze pierced through me with a mixture of hope and dread. "Or was that just said to reach whatever was left of me?"

I swallowed, and it was my turn to look away. A part of me didn't want to admit to the adoration I felt for him. It was much easier to admit my feelings when I thought we were both doomed.

"Kylee?" he asked, drawing my gaze back to his.

"Yes." My answer was quiet and small. "I meant it."

He leaned back on the couch, relief smoothing the lines in his face. "I thought you might have been feeding me some bullshit just to survive." He glanced at his soiled shirt and my bloodstained bathing suit. "I need to get some clean clothes on." He stood and held out his hand. "Come on."

I took his hand and let him lead me downstairs to the bedroom we hadn't been in together since the first day of this catastrophic cruise. He led me into the shower and turned the water on, pulling me inside with him.

Neither of us had cleaned up since we left California, and the hot water stream felt like heaven until I turned my back into it. I winced as my cuts took a direct hit.

Alex quickly washed himself with the body wash and shampoo and then did the same to me, taking care to avoid getting soap directly in my cuts. The water ran red for longer than I cared to see, but it soon turned pink and then clear. He shampooed my hair twice, and it felt like I had entered nirvana. His fingers were gentle and soft as they kneaded my scalp.

After I was all clean, he turned me towards him and wrapped his arms around me, bringing me to his chest.

"Thank you for saving me," he whispered in my ear. "I know what you had to sacrifice in order to do that."

I hugged him back, the numbness of my actions thawing, and with it came the tears. Tears mourning my brother's death, mourning all the death and destruction he created. Alex held tight while I cried. When all my tears dried up, I pulled out of his grasp.

He shut the water off and wrapped a towel around his waist. He grabbed the second towel and dried me off before he turned me around to inspect my back.

"I think you might need stitches for a couple of these." His finger traced my skin between cuts, then he opened the medicine cabinet.

"The first aid kit is in the bathroom upstairs," I said as he shuffled through the cabinets in the bathroom.

"Just wait here. I'll be right back." He stepped out of the room.

I sat on the toilet seat waiting for him, letting the numbness take hold of both my mind and my body. When he came back, he wore shorts and a T-shirt. He pulled me into the bedroom where he had the entire first aid kit laid out on the bed. He pulled the vanity stool over and sat me down on it before working on my back.

He dabbed something cool and soothing on the burning cuts and I sighed.

"So what do we do now?" he asked as he continued to work on patching me up the best he could.

I remained quiet, mulling it over. I wasn't sure if he was asking about us or our current situation, so I went with the safer bet. "I have no idea how we're going to get this boat back to port and explain the loss of the crew and the condition of the cabin upstairs."

He huffed a laugh. "I wasn't asking about the fucked up predicament we are in."

"Oh."

He turned the stool, so I faced him and continued patching the front of my shoulder. Once he had the bandage in place, he met my gaze.

"How does this work?" He pointed between the two of us.

"You know what I am and what I've done. But you don't know everything." I stood and rifled through my suitcase, pulling on a pair of shorts and a comfortable loose tank top before I turned to him. "If there is ever going to be anything more between us, you need to know what my deal is."

He closed up the first aid kit and patted the corner of the bed next to where he sat. His expression was neutral. Unreadable.

"I have a paranormal investigation agency, but that's not what I'm doing here. This trip was something I was ordered to do."

"By who?" he asked cautiously.

"Fate. I work for her as a kind of bounty hunter."

"Fate?" He laughed at me like I was shoveling shit in his direction.

The air shifted, and I cringed. I had hoped I wouldn't have to deal with Fate until I got home. Alex shot to his feet and stepped back into the side table. His eyes widened at the vision of the queen bitch herself. I stood, putting myself between her and Alex. The tight set of her lips and the blaze in her eyes left me shaking.

Her signature red dress billowed as she pointed her finger at me. "You violated the rules," she growled.

"I did what you said. I killed my own flesh and blood." My teeth clicked closed so tight that my jaw hurt.

"You employed your siren," she spat back.

I nodded. "Twice. But no innocents died as a result."

Her hands balled into fists. "I should drag your ass back to Lucifer right now," she said with all the fire and fury written on her face.

Alex's hands curled around my shoulders. "I don't think so." He held on to me like I could be yanked from his life at the whim of the woman standing before him, which was an accurate assessment.

Her fiery gaze moved from mine to his. "She also violated her contract by telling you about our deal." She crossed her arms. "So what punishment do *you* deem fitting for breaking the rules?"

Alex stared Fate down, blissfully unafraid of the woman. "She killed her own brother. What more do you want from her?"

"Do whatever you want to me, but leave him alone," I said as a hot flash of panic filled my form. My heart jumped into my throat, pounding hard enough to make breathing as difficult as it had been after my brother crushed my ribs.

Fate was a fickle bitch, and she could yank him out of my life just as easily as she could yank me back to hell. And she enjoyed tormenting me. I wouldn't put anything past her right now, especially with the lack of fear coming from Alex.

She stepped closer, glaring down at me.

"If you so much as harm a hair on his head, I'll open so many goddamned portals that this earth will be overrun by monsters, and you will not have your little bounty hunter to clean up the mess." The ultimatum slipped out of my mouth in a feral growl. After all the shit she had put me through, if she yanked Alex from this world to spite me, I would do damage on a cataclysmic scale.

Fate blinked at the venom in my voice, and perhaps she heard the truth in my words because she took a step back, distancing herself. Her eyes narrowed as she studied me. She pulled a book out of her skirt ruffles and ran her perfectly manicured nail down each page before she flipped to the other side, continuing page after page while we waited for her sentence. She slammed the book closed and glared at me, sliding the book back into her pockets.

"You are a lucky girl. The people who died on your watch were already on death's list, and he isn't." Her gaze moved beyond me to Alex and back. "But I cannot let your transgression go unpunished." An evil smile spread across her lips.

I went to speak, but she reached out with her hand and yanked at the air, pulling her fist tight. My body jerked, and I inhaled at the sudden release from my throat. For a moment, I thought she'd cut it wide open, but then Fate held her hand over a vial. Light filled the glass, and she corked it.

"That should teach you," Fate purred before she blinked out, leaving a swirl of smoke in her place.

My legs turned to jelly, and I took an unsteady step before sitting on the side of the bed.

"She's quite the bitch." Alex crouched down in front of me. "Why don't you tell her to go pound sand?"

I met his gaze and opened my mouth. No sound came out. My hand went to my throat. The skin was intact, but I could no longer speak. Fate had left me a mute. She stole my damn voice.

"Kylee?"

I pointed to my throat.

His eyes grew. "What did she do?"

I tapped my throat and waved bye-bye.

"She took your voice?"

I nodded and closed my eyes, hanging my head. I took a breath and gathered my wits. Lots of people existed with less.

Do you know sign language? I signed slowly, hoping I had the gestures correct.

He just stared at my hands. I could have been signing ancient Greek to him for all he knew. I'd have to teach him how to read what I was saying, but in the meantime, we had more pressing issues to attend to. Like how to explain the condition of the boat and not end up rotting somewhere in jail in Greece for the rest of our lives.

Chapter 15

WE STOOD LOOKING AT the dingy in the cargo hold. It was one of those nice proactive lifeboats. The inflatable one Alex had used as my healing tub wasn't the only one on board. I was glad the captain had given us a full tour of the boat before we set sail, because otherwise I would have never dreamed up this plan.

"Are you sure?" Alex asked.

I nodded and typed a message to him on his tablet. *It's the only plausible way for us to get out of this.*

We had hashed out every other scenario, from cruising into harbor with the boat as is, to calling for help, and everything in between. Our only hope of being let on the plane home was to get into the lifeboat and head back with the story that we escaped when pirates took over the yacht. It weaved the truth together and would explain quite a lot if any of the bodies or boats were found. Every other scenario landed us in a jail cell.

"It's risky. They might find this boat before we get to shore," Alex said, rubbing his chin. "But maybe if they do, it will lend credence to our story."

I think the bizarre massacre on the cruise ship might help our situation too. Let's see what we can gather. We are close to two hundred miles southeast of Crete, so in all likelihood, we are looking at five days in that thing before we hit land. I finished typing, handed him the tablet, and turned my back on our escape route, heading back into the belly of the boat.

"We can't fare too well," he said. "Escaping in a well-equipped dingy is kind of suspect."

I paused at the door and nodded. I hoped there wasn't anything he was attached to in his suitcase. I just needed to make sure we had enough food and water to survive an extended time in that little boat.

I did a walk-through on the main floor and grabbed an armful of waters, as well as a couple handfuls of snacks, before heading to the bedroom. I emptied my backpack and dropped my broken charm bracelet in the inside pocket before placing the water and snacks in the bag. From my suitcase, I grabbed a change of clothing and did the same for Alex.

I started to leave and then turned back, grabbing our wallets, phones, and passports and shoved them in the same pocket as my bracelet. I hesitated at the doorway, thinking about my patch job. I grabbed the first aid kit, and with the bag, headed back to the cargo hold and Alex waiting with the boat now in the water.

"This thing has a sail," he said with a smile and glanced at the two things I held. "What did you end up grabbing?"

I opened the backpack to show him our stash.

"Clothes?"

I nodded and put the tablet in the bag as well. I hoped the battery lasted more than a few hours. It was the only efficient way to communicate with Alex.

"I wouldn't have thought of that." He reached his hand out to take the bag.

I handed it over, along with the first aid kit, and then let him help me in the boat. He climbed in and pushed off, glancing at the luxury yacht with a sigh.

"It's such a shame," he mumbled and took a seat next to me on the bench, handing me one of the oars.

We rowed in tandem, watching as the boat drew farther and farther away. Neither of us spoke or typed. We just watched as the sun breached the horizon, coloring the sky. Our slow row was hypnotizing. We kept it until the sun rose higher in the sky.

"I need some water," Alex said.

His voice reflected the scratchy dryness that my mouth held. We both pulled our oars in, and I unzipped the backpack, pulling out two water bottles and handing him one. I reached in again and pulled out a couple of protein bars, which we both tore into just as heartily as the water.

"When did we last eat?" he asked after he inhaled the food and drained half the bottle of water.

Yesterday morning, before the pirates boarded. I typed on his tablet and handed it to him. I returned my attention to my water, taking small sips to savor the liquid.

"Shit. No wonder I'm a little dizzy," Alex said as he hoisted the dingy sail.

He adjusted the angle so our heading continued to the northwest. Then he settled in the seat next to me, drinking the remainder of his water in the same conserving sips I was taking.

The wind picked up, moving us along at a decent clip. He didn't feel the need to fill the silence with talk. He just sat holding my hand as we moved back towards civilization. Thankfully, we were in the Mediterranean, which was fairly calm in relation to the open Pacific. Not that there weren't strong currents or bad weather; it was just less prevalent than in the open ocean where one can go thousands of miles without sight of land. The widest point between land masses was less than a thousand miles. Where we were, unless we started drifting due west, we only had four hundred miles between Greece and Egypt, and we had been dead center when we left the yacht behind.

"I'm in need of a nap," Alex said, meeting my gaze. "Can you man the helm while I catch a little shut-eye, and then I'll cover you?" Dark circles under his eyes punctuated his exhaustion.

I nodded and traded places, taking the rudder from him to make sure we kept on our track. I wasn't tired in the least. Something about sailing quietly on the water had invigorated me. Besides, the cuts on my abdomen, back, and shoulder would probably make sleep impossible.

He leaned over and placed a kiss on my cheek. "Wake me if something happens." He crawled under the canopy at the front of the dingy. He was snoring within minutes.

I let him sleep until the sun dropped on the horizon. Along with the twilight came exhaustion, and my head bobbed. I jerked in place, forcing myself to stay awake long enough to hand over the post.

I kicked Alex's foot, and he shot up, nearly banging his head on the canvas canopy.

"What?" Panic laced his question as his gaze darted left and right. When it landed on me, he stared as if he wasn't sure where he was. He rubbed his face and glanced at the darkening sky. "You let me sleep all day?"

I nodded and yawned.

He climbed out of the hull and took over steering while I crawled to where he had been and attempted to find a comfortable position. The minute I closed my eyes, my eyelids acted like a deranged movie plex where the last few days kept flashing over and over until I thought I'd scream.

I finally silenced the angst and drifted into a restless slumber. In my dream, the trident pierced Alex's heart, and my brother drove a stake through mine. We died on that pole together until Fate came and dragged me by the hair, kicking and screaming all the way into Lucifer's lair.

My penance in hell wasn't being Lucifer's whore. No. It was much worse. My voice was taken from me, and I couldn't utter a sound. And then they put me in a room where I had to watch as Alex was slowly torn to pieces in front of me.

"Kylee!"

Alex's voice broke through the nightmare as his hands shook me awake. I opened my eyes and flew into his arms, nearly knocking both of us over the edge of the dingy.

"Hey," he whispered in my ear as I clung to him like a frightened kid. "It's okay. It's all over."

I would have thought I'd be the one consoling him after our encounter. Especially since he'd had no beliefs in the supernatural less than a week ago. He seemed to have rolled with this much smoother than anyone in my past.

I pulled away and brought my hand to his cheek. The smoothness that had been there this morning after our shower was now marred with prickly stubble.

It was just a nightmare. I typed out on his tablet.

"I was surprised I wasn't plagued with them all day," he said. "Did you want me to drop anchor and hold you so you can get some sleep?"

I leaned back, studying him before typing. *I'm not a damsel in distress.*

His lips pressed together in a smirk, and he looked out at the water. "I never insinuated that you were," he said, while trying not to smile at me. "I just thought..." He met my gaze. "I don't know what I was thinking," he admitted with a laugh. "I keep forgetting you've been around longer than I have. I was just trying to offer you some comfort."

That's very sweet, but I'm not sure you holding me would help with the nightmares.

He glanced at my words. "Okay, do you want to tell me about it at all?"

I shook my head and cuddled next to him on the bench. I picked up the bottle of water at his feet and took a sip before returning it to its spot. We had been on the sea for less than twenty-four hours and had cracked open the third bottle.

We might need to slow down on the water. I typed and looked up at the sail as it barely flopped in place. *We have at least two more full days.*

"Which means you need to get some actual sleep. We have to alternate in order to cross the distance as quickly as possible." He folded the sail. It wasn't doing much with relatively little wind. He tossed the anchor overboard. "I don't expect us to get very far without wind, and I don't have the energy to row alone, so we are going to get more sleep and conserve some energy in case we have to do some rowing in the morning. Okay?"

I couldn't argue with his logic, so I let him pull me down onto the hard hull. His shoulder made for a soft pillow, and the heat from his body kept me warm. I closed my eyes and thought, *Just for a few minutes.*

Chapter 16

HOLY BRIGHTNESS. I TURNED my head away from the light and into a hard knob. I blinked my eyes open and stared at an elbow. It took me a moment to place where I was, and I nearly chuckled. The only thing that stopped the laugh from escaping was the origin of the light. It wasn't the sun. It was a spotlight.

I shook Alex awake. His groggy gaze met mine, then squinted into the light. He shot to a sitting position, scraping his head on the canopy in his haste to get up. The person holding the light lowered it a fraction. Beyond the bright spot sat another small craft.

"Είσαι καλά?" a voice called from beyond the light.

Alex traded a glance with me. While I understood the question asked in Greek, he obviously didn't, and without a voice, I couldn't answer.

"Are you okay?" the voice asked in English this time.

"Who are you?" Alex asked in a wary voice.

"Coast Guard," the man said.

The tenseness in Alex's form released, and he slumped. "Thank God," he said. "We're banged up, and she needs stitches. I did the best I could to fix her up before we escaped, but I'm not a doctor."

The skiff closed the distance, and someone tied a rope to the pad eye of our lifeboat before they pulled alongside us.

Alex helped me to my feet, and just before he handed me over to the Coast Guard, I pointed towards the backpack, meeting his gaze.

"Don't worry. I won't forget what little we have left." He gave me a tired smile.

I crossed over into the skiff with the help of three military-built men in uniforms.

"What's your name?" the one holding my arm asked.

I glanced at him and tapped my throat with a shake of my head.

"She hasn't spoken since we were attacked on the yacht we rented," Alex said as he stepped into the skiff with the backpack hanging over his shoulder.

A flashlight shined at my throat, and the owner of the light actually winced. I hadn't had cause to really study myself in a mirror since my brother died, but I ventured from the man's face that I had some nasty bruises from when Jeremiah tried to strangle me to death. A crushed larynx would be a hell of a reasonable fabrication, and I was glad Alex's explanation spawned the thought. It certainly would explain my loss of voice.

"We'll get you to a doctor in no time," the man said after he shut off the light. He sat me on a bench and wrapped a warm blanket around my shoulders.

Alex took a seat next to me with a blanket wrapped around him, too. He put the backpack between his feet and threaded his hand in mine. The simple gesture warmed me more than the blanket.

They brought us to a bigger cruiser, helped us aboard, and brought us into a sheltered area while they headed toward Greece's mainland.

A formal looking gentleman in a neatly pressed uniform came in and took a seat across from us. He pulled out a pen, scribbled on the clipboard he held, and then finally looked up at us.

"I am Commander Angelis with the Hellenic Coast Guard."

His heavy Greek accent was hard to miss, and the fact he remained all business sent off alarms in my head. I gave him a nod and traded a glance with Alex.

"I'm Alejandro Cervas, and this is Kylee Paradox." Alex put his hand out, and the commander stared at it for a moment before he shook it. The pause was enough to set the mood. This would not be a pleasant conversation.

"Were you aware that Captain Hagan and his crew were murdered?"

I stared at him and slowly nodded. Alex hadn't been conscious when the captain died. I made a motion for something to write on, and the commander handed me a pen and paper.

We were attacked by something; I wrote. If they found the boat, the crusted statue of my brother would go a long way to substantiate the partial truth I was spinning. *Alex played dead, and before the something killed me, another boat came into the vicinity, and the thing took off. But before it left, it promised it would be back for me.*

I glanced at Alex, and he gave me a nod before I handed the commander the paper.

Commander Angelis raised an eyebrow as he read my note. "You expect me to believe this?"

I stood and let the blanket drop from my shoulders so I could lift my shirt, showing him the deep gashes Jeremiah's nails left. And then I turned so he could see the same on my back. I pulled the shirt down and took a seat.

Alex draped the blanket around me again. "It did that to her," he said, meeting the commander's sharp gaze. "Whatever the hell *it* was."

The commander leaned forward and handed the paper back to me. "What did you do next?"

Alex started to answer, and the commander glared at him. "I want to hear this from her."

I glanced at Alex, then held the pen to the paper once again. *We ran. That thing took the bodies with him into the sea and took off. I wasn't waiting around for him to come back and finish us. We lifted anchor and headed away as fast as the yacht would take us. Unfortunately, we didn't get very far before pirates attacked the ship.*

I handed the sheet to him and waved my fingers for more. He handed me another piece. Before I continued, my hand fluttered to my throat, and I blinked back the mist that covered my eyes.

The pirates... Well, they wanted to sell me to the highest bidder back home, but wanted to make sure I'd be worth the money. They nearly killed me before the men turned on each other. It gave us the opportunity to escape. We'd been drifting in that lifeboat for a few days.

I handed the last sheet to the commander and avoided eye contact. This was the dicey part. If they didn't believe us, we were going to be screwed for a very long time.

He read the note, closed his eyes, and wiped his face before clearing his throat.

"And where were you during all this?" he asked Alex, his voice as accusatory as it had been before.

"I was in and out of consciousness for part of it and then just blazing mad. But Kylee kept me out of harm's way and got me down to where the lifeboat was. Her voice was gone by that point, but she was able to get me to understand we needed to escape. We left just as gunfire broke out in the main cabin."

He studied us, his gaze traveling from Alex to me and back like he was measuring the level of bullshit we were feeding him. There was something under the accusation in his eyes. Something haunting. I had an epiphany and pointed at the papers. He handed me one.

I wrote, *How many men on this ship died?*

When I handed him the slip of paper, he recoiled, his eyes widening before shooting to mine. His composure melted, and he crumpled the paper and looked away.

This man was looking for answers. Answers as to why his ship became a war zone. A mythological creature wasn't good enough. Especially since he himself had been affected by my brother's siren song. There were too many haunting glances at me not to be right about this.

I tapped the floor with my foot, bringing his attention back to me.

"Six," he answered and paled. "One by my own hand, and I need to know why."

An ensign came in, interrupting the conversation. He handed the commander a photograph. Commander Angelis stared at the picture for a good minute before his gaze rose. Whatever color had remained on his face faded, leaving him almost green. He blinked, glanced up at the ensign, and handed me the photo.

"Was this on the yacht when you boarded?" he asked with a tremble in his voice.

I looked at the black-and-white photo of Jeremiah frozen in death. A shiver rippled through me, and I dropped the photo as if it were burning my fingers. My hand went to my throat. I shook my head, trying to swallow the bile that had risen in my esophagus. The revulsion and horror filling my form hit like a fastball to the abdomen.

Alex put his arm around me. "That was the thing that nearly killed us," he said, staring at the photo face up on the floor.

I glanced at his pale profile. His aversion to the photo was as real as mine. I could feel it in his grip on my shoulder and see it in the tension of his jaw. When he raised his gaze to the commander, the man across from us flinched.

Commander Angelis ran his hand over his face. "That is a statue," he said, denying what he must know as the truth.

In these parts, there was plenty of speculation regarding mermaids and sirens. Especially after what happened to that cruise ship.

"It wasn't when we saw it, and it had legs, not the damn tail you see in that picture. The face is the same, and so are the clawed hands," Alex snapped. "If you have any doubts, measure the statue's damn hand and compare it to the bruise on her neck." He hooked his thumb in my direction. "Or measure the spread of the thing's claws and compare them to the cuts on her stomach and back if you still have doubts."

The commander's gaze moved to my throat. "If you wouldn't mind putting your hand over the shape of the bruise," he said to Alex.

"Excuse me?"

"Do it," he snarled.

I lifted my chin and turned toward Alex. His hand was much smaller than my brother's, so I had no issue with the request. At least it might ease the obvious angst the commander had in relation to us.

Alex did as he asked. The commander mumbled under his breath.

"Thank you." He picked up the paper from the floor and waved the ensign guarding the door over.

I caught the whisper to have someone measure the hand on the statue and for the ensign to measure the mark on my throat. He gave a nod and stepped out. When he returned, he had a piece of string that he used to span the bruise. With the length measured, he left us alone with the commander.

"I don't believe in mythology..." Commander Angelis stood, glancing out over the ocean. "But I heard the most haunting songs before all hell broke out on this ship. It was like what you described happened to those pirates. And if I allow myself to believe for a second that a merman did this to all of us, I will be put in a padded room for a very long time." He turned to us. "Why did we stop? Why didn't we slaughter ourselves until everyone was dead like on that cruise ship?"

I pointed at the picture and made the writing motion. He handed me another piece of paper.

If that truly is the being that attacked us, perhaps his death released us all from the siren's control.

He stared at my note and then met my gaze. "You heard the song?"

Both of us nodded.

His expression hardened. "You killed the crew members of that boat?"

We both shook our heads.

"The crew attacked Kylee." Alex looked at the ground and closed his eyes. "I did, too. She defended herself pretty well, considering four men were on the attack, but neither of us killed the crew. She did her best to keep us from harming her or each other. I guess that thing wasn't satisfied with how things were playing out and decided to take things into its own hands."

The commander glanced at me, his eyes narrowing. "You were not affected?"

I shook my head and grabbed another piece of paper. *No, not in the same way the men were. I tied the captain and Alex up to keep them safe. That creature snapped the necks of the other two and then let the captain loose with instructions to kill me. Alex was already unconscious. When I nearly knocked the Captain out, that thing got angry, broke the captain's neck, and came after me. Just before he did the same to me, another ship came into the vicinity.*

I stopped writing and looked up at the commander. My heart sunk. It was his ship that made it so my life was spared. I handed him the paper as tears welled up in my eyes. Six crew members paid the price instead of me.

He read my words and then met my gaze. I pointed a shaky finger at him and twirled it around to indicate the ship. The truth of it all slammed home, and I buried my face in my hands. If I had only killed Jeremiah that first time, the commander's ship wouldn't have been influenced by the siren.

Commander Angelis kneeled down in front of me and pulled my hands from my face. I met his gaze through prisms of tears. The hardness in his features softened.

"I think that may have been us, and to know our arrival saved two people from death is more than I could have hoped for."

I glanced at Alex, and he squeezed me to his side.

"Thank you," Alex said. He relayed the depth of my gratitude with those two words.

The commander gave a nod, climbed to his feet, and left us alone.

"I'm sorry, Kylee," Alex said softly, and pressed his lips to the side of my head.

I wasn't sure why he was apologizing, but I accepted his warm condolences.

THE COMMANDER AND CREW let us be for the remainder of the trip. Neither Alex nor I got any rest, and we didn't talk. I just leaned into him, thankful for his warmth and quiet strength. Numbness settled into my bones, taking any discomfort from my injuries.

We arrived in Athens just as the sun kissed the surface of the sea.

"Miss?" an ensign said, sticking his head in the room we sat in.

I met his gaze and raised an eyebrow.

"We have medics waiting on shore to take a look at you."

I glanced at Alex. I just wanted to go home.

"You need to get your back looked at before we get on a plane," he said, as if he read my mind.

I sighed and nodded. I climbed to my feet and took an unsteady step. Alex grabbed my elbow, steadying me before he grabbed our backpack. The minute we climbed onto the dock, a medic swept in and escorted both of us into the nearest building on the base.

I was given a johnny to put on. They tried to remove Alex from the room, but I kept his hand in mine and shook my head.

"I'm staying," he said.

"We need to check you out too," the medic said.

I pointed to the floor in the room, still clasping his hand.

"She wants me to stay. I don't have an issue if you check me out in front of her. And if I'm reading her correctly, she feels the same."

I nodded, thankful for his accurate interpretation of my actions.

"Fine." The medic handed Alex a johnny as well. "Get changed and the doctor will be in momentarily."

Alex helped me out of my shirt and into the garment, then he traded his shirt for the johnny and took a seat next to me on the bench. He didn't bother asking if I was okay. I thought by then he knew better, so instead, he took my hand in his and gave it a squeeze.

I returned the motion as the doctor walked into the room. She was a beautiful, dark-haired Greek woman, and she gave me a soft smile.

"Hello, I'm Doctor Romanov. I understand you haven't spoken since the attack," she said, looking at some notes scribbled on the clipboard she held. It was strange not seeing a doctor with a tablet like in the states, but perhaps they weren't as advanced as that here on the coast guard base.

I nodded and lifted my chin to show my neck.

Dr. Romanov put the clipboard down and crossed to me. Concern displayed in tiny wrinkles around her mouth. She pressed lightly on either side of my Adam's apple. I winced. She made me stick my tongue out while she flashed a light down my throat, but I knew there was no actual sign of damage. Fate had just stolen my ability to speak, and no medical doctor could restore it.

"Did you cough up blood?" she asked.

I shook my head and glanced at Alex.

"No, she didn't," he said. "I think her back and shoulder need more attention at the moment than her throat," he added as the doctor kept tinkering with my neck. "I did my best to patch her up, but I still think stitches are necessary."

The doctor glanced at him before returning her gaze to me. "Does it hurt to swallow?"

I shook my head, then shrugged and pointed to the sides of my neck. I signed the muscles were sore, but not my throat directly.

"Your muscles are sore?"

I nodded. *You know sign language?*

She stared at my hands and gave me a nod. "Yes. As far as the muscles in your neck, they will be sore for a while. You sustained some really nasty bruises." Her glance jumped to Alex in a manner I didn't like.

He saved me, I signed. *So don't give him that look. He's got a head injury, if you hadn't noticed.*

Dr. Romanov took a long breath. "Okay. Let's look at your back." She walked to the other side of the table. She pulled off the patchwork that Alex had done. "Your boyfriend is right. You are going to need quite a few stitches."

I traded a glance with Alex, and he shrugged.

"I told you it wasn't pretty." He squeezed my hand.

"I wouldn't talk, mister. That bruise on your forehead is pretty nasty." The doctor stepped around to the front of me.

"I'm fine," Alex said. "I just need about thirty hours of sleep after I eat a four-course meal."

His comment brought a smile to my lips. It had the same effect on the doctor as she shined her light in each of his eyes.

She returned to me and slid the johnny off my shoulder to inspect that wound. When she finished, she met my gaze. "You are one lucky lady. It looks like this missed the tendons and just hit bone. If this had been a half inch in either direction, you wouldn't have been able to use this arm. At least not enough to keep fighting whatever attacked you two."

I shrugged and glanced at Alex. *I'm not sure I could have kept fighting if it wasn't for him,* I signed.

The doctor nodded. "I'll be back with the nurse, and we will get you sewed up."

Thank you.

Dr. Romanov and the nurse who had got us settled in the exam room worked together to stitch up my shoulder and the gouges in my back. They then sent us on our way with enough bandages to get us home to the states. I stopped at the marina store and bought both Alex and me some flip-flops for our feet before we got into the cab that the base had called for us.

I leaned back in the seat and winced. Any pressure on my back pulled at the stitches. I leaned forward enough so my back didn't press on the vinyl. Alex slid inside next to me with the backpack.

"Where to?" he asked softly.

Airport, I mouthed and made the hand signal for an airplane taking off.

"The airport, please," Alex said to the driver without hesitation.

While he didn't know formal sign language, he was reading me pretty damn well, and I was thankful for that.

The cab driver dropped us off and waved away payment, telling us the coast guard had covered the cost before he drove away. Alex and I turned and took in the airport, and I wondered if there was even a flight today.

When the airline clerk told us there wasn't anything until tomorrow morning, I almost burst into tears. I nodded and wrote a note to please book us on the earliest flight possible, then I handed over my credit card to cover the charges for both of us.

"I assume there's a hotel in connection with the airport?" Alex asked after our tickets were all squared away.

"Yes." She pointed to our right. "If you go through the doors at the end of this hall, you will come to a passageway that connects with the hotel."

"Thank you." He took the tickets and my hand and led me away from the airport terminal.

I felt like a walking zombie, numb except for the discomfort of my back. I let Alex take charge. He booked us a room and got me settled under the covers before he slid into the bed next to me. I remembered nothing beyond his soft peck on my lips and then the shifting of the covers before darkness yanked me under.

Chapter 17

RINGING YANKED ME OUT of a sound sleep, and I rolled, wincing at the pain in my back. I glanced around the room and at the empty spot beside me, disoriented. My attention finally turned back to the nightstand next to me and the buzzing phone. I picked up the receiver and got an automated wake-up message.

Alex stepped out of the bathroom with a towel wrapped around his waist and rubbed his wet hair with a second towel. "Hey, sleepyhead." He flashed a smile. "Was that our wake-up call?"

I nodded and tried to stretch, but the movement pulled a silent gasp from my lips.

"You might want to clean up and change before we go sit on a plane for another eighteen hours." He sighed and stepped back in the bathroom. "Thank you for having the forethought to grab a change of clothes," he called from behind the door.

They had said for me to wait at least twenty-four hours before I took a shower, but I needed to feel clean after everything we had been through. As soon as Alex vacated the bathroom, I slid inside and turned on the shower.

"They said to wait a full day," Alex said from the doorway.

I turned and sent him a glare, daring him to stop me. He raised his hands and stepped out of sight. I left the bandages on until I finished cleaning my body and hair. The adhesive peeled off easily, and once I had all the bandages I could reach removed, I wrapped my hair in a towel and loosely draped the other around my body.

I stepped into the room, and Alex looked up. I pointed at him and then turned so he could remove the last soaking bandage I couldn't reach. He pulled the fabric away from my skin, took the towel I held, and blotted the skin in between each cut.

The man had such a delicate touch that I closed my eyes.

"Do you need me to put the spare bandages on?" he asked softly in my ear.

His proximity stirred a need deep within me. It was the first emotion I'd had since we stepped off the coast guard boat. I nodded, not because I couldn't patch myself up, but because I just wanted him near me. I needed to feel something more than this vast emptiness that had overtaken me.

Once my wounds were covered, he handed me my clean clothing. I took them with me back to the bathroom, dressing and finishing the motions of cleaning up. Thankfully, the hotel supplied us with toothbrushes, toothpaste, and deodorant, so at least I felt human when I stepped out of the bathroom.

Neither of us bothered to pick up our dirty clothing. I think we both just wanted to get home and leave all reminders of what had passed behind. I handed him his wallet and his passport from the backpack before pointing at the door.

"You're in a rush." He pocketed his documents before hooking his thumb at the cart of food behind him. "Didn't you want something to eat?"

I shook my head. I wasn't hungry. I hadn't been since the numbness took hold.

"You need to eat something." He picked up the apple and tossed it to me as he folded a pancake and shoved it into his mouth. He wiped his hands on a napkin while chewing and swallowing the pastry. "Ready?"

I nodded and took a bite of the apple. The juicy sweetness soothed my throat. I knew at some point I'd be thankful he insisted I eat something, but as we left the room, I tossed the half-eaten fruit in the garbage and closed the door. My mood soured with each uncomfortable step.

As soon as we settled our bill, I headed straight to the airport terminal. I wanted away from this side of the world and the memories that would haunt me for the next thousand millenniums thanks to that demanding bitch. And now I couldn't even have a decent conversation because of her slanted view of justice.

Thousands of years had passed since I found joy in destroying a human life, and I had lost all taste for it. In a way, I was glad Fate stole my voice, but it really wasn't necessary. I would never again engage the siren. Not at the expense of a life. Using it to lull my brother had been enough to kill that urge on the spot.

Alex tried to engage me in conversation, but I tuned him out, preferring to wallow in what might have been as opposed to the cold reality that I killed Jeremiah. Once we were seated on the plane, I closed my eyes.

"Kylee?" he whispered. He took my hand in his and gave it a squeeze. "You did the right thing."

I took his iPad and typed, *I know. But it still doesn't fix the hole his death left in my heart.*

Alex leaned over and planted a soft kiss on my cheek. "If there is anything I can do to ease your pain, please let me know."

I stared out the window and then grabbed his iPad back. *We need to learn sign language because this typing shit is for the birds.*

"Well, we have close to nineteen hours trapped in this fuselage, and I know neither of us is in the mood for a repeat of the prior trip, so..." He handed me the iPad. "Have at it."

Chapter 18

WE WALKED INTO MY home, and Alex dropped the backpack on the kitchen island. I fished through it and pulled my bracelet out.

"What are you doing?" Alex asked.

I yanked the trident off the chain and held it up, meeting his gaze. *I need you to say the spell that returns this to normal size.* I signed slowly. He had picked up a lot in the nineteen hours we were stuck on the flight, but I still had to go slow enough for him to process it.

His mouth moved as he translated what my hands were saying. "You need me to say a spell?"

I nodded and scribbled it down. I hesitated before I handed him the note. I could see him testing out the spell and one or both of us being speared by the trident as a result. *But wait until we get upstairs and I tell you to say the spell, okay?*

He nodded. "I'll wait until you give me the go ahead," he said, and I handed him the paper.

Alex studied the words as he followed me up to my weapons arsenal. Thankfully, I didn't use a voice-controlled code for access. Otherwise, I'd be screwed. As it was, I would need Alex to recount whatever spell was necessary to use my tools, or I'd be shit out of luck the next time I had to go take down a monster.

I pressed the code into the door and positioned myself in front of the scanner. Alex let out a low whistle.

"Impressive," he said after the lock disengaged.

I crossed to the long dresser and laid my hands on the specific spots needed to open the secret cabinet and waited, relishing the heat that flowed into my hands from the scanners. The audible click announced the completion of the process, and I opened the dresser lid. I dropped the trinket in the center of the velvet holder and glanced over my shoulder. Alex stared into the cabinet in appreciation at the array of knives, daggers, and other deadly weapons.

"Damn, girl." He met my gaze. The utter appreciation reflected in his eyes made me shift. I didn't deserve idolization.

I rolled my eyes and tapped the paper in his hand.

"Oh, yeah." He cleared his throat and repeated the words on the paper. His pronunciation was off, so nothing happened.

I bit my lip. *Do you remember how I said it on the boat?*

He stared at my hands, and the color in his cheeks faded a notch. He closed his eyes. His lips moved, but no sound came out at first. Then his eyes flew open, and he spoke the exact words I used after he had collapsed. *"Deus Neptunus in mari nascuntur tridentem istum mihi."*

Light flashed over the trident, and we both squinted as it grew to its full glory. Seeing the dried blood covering the forks, and the handle sucked the air from my lungs. I plucked the note from Alex's hand and dropped it into the case before I slammed the top closed.

I grabbed his hand and literally dragged him from the room, slamming the door behind us. I leaned against it, still trying to draw a full breath, but my lungs didn't seem to be on the same page.

"Kylee?"

I turned and signed, *Thank you.*

His goofy, uncomfortable smile appeared. "Any time," he said. "I guess."

We stood staring at each other, and his smile faded. My heart dropped at the seriousness of his expression. It was as if he were seeing me for the first time. I thought it was doubt I glimpsed, but then he moved, pinning me to the door.

His lips captured mine, and he kissed like a drowning man clawing his way to the surface. It was frantic and full of everything he had held back since my brother died. His hands gripped my arms, harder than I thought he intended. When he finally broke the kiss, the intensity in his gaze reminded me of what he looked like on the boat just before he ravaged me.

I shivered and kept his stare.

"I want to do this right this time," he said, his voice husky with the need so obvious in the hardness now pressed against me.

I didn't have a witty response, especially since my hands were down at my sides. I wanted to say something like there was no helm for me to spray, or if he wanted me to bend over. I wanted to say anything to keep this intensity from burning out.

Instead, I broke his grip on my arms and yanked him back to my lips. I needed this as much as he did, and the pain of my injuries only heightened my desire to wipe out all conscious thought.

He whisked me off my feet, and I pointed towards my bedroom. He didn't need to be told twice. In my room, our clothing came off in such a flurry, I thought we might have charged the air. The electrical current between the two of us reached the insanity level bordering on combustion.

He pushed me back onto the bed and kneeled on the floor, pulling me until my knees rested on his shoulders. Just the mere thought of his tongue inside me created a warmth through my entire form.

The frantic pace at which our clothing came off halted. He grinned as his tongue traced the inside of my thigh from my knee to my hip joint. He did the same with my other leg before kissing my stomach. Each time he avoided my pussy, my breath hitched.

He navigated my abdomen up to my breasts, using his hands and mouth to tease me. He knew what I wanted, but he was hell bent on taking his time. I had no voice to protest. I was at his mercy, and what a sweet mercy it was.

He kissed me, rolling his tongue with mine in such a sweet ride that I sighed into it. Then he traveled back to where he started. With a sparkle in his deep brown eyes, he lowered his head and sucked my sensitive nub. His tongue started a dance that left me panting.

His fingers breached my core, sliding in and out with such a patient slowness that if I'd had a voice, I would have screamed. When he finally pulled away, the emptiness caught my breath.

"Roll onto your knees," he said in a commanding tone, one I couldn't deny.

The minute my ass was in the air, he grabbed hold of my hips and slid inside me. His stroke was slow, so slow I thought I was going to lose my mind. The lack of being able to purr my satisfaction frustrated me, heightening every sensation.

His hand traveled from my waist to my clit, and his damn fingers started that slow roll, bringing me to the next level. I had a feeling I knew what was coming. When he slipped out and into my ass, I hissed air between my teeth.

He slowly pushed his entire length inside and then pulled me to his chest. His fingers kept playing with my clit, and his other hand rolled the hard nubs of my breasts between his thumb and forefinger, creating a delicious heat that nearly undid me.

"Cum for me, Kylee," he whispered in my ear. His hips started their circular roll, creating such heat inside my core that if I'd had my siren voice, it would have been released without my permission.

This was too good to be true. Too pure to last, but I reached back and grabbed his hips, forcing him to move faster and harder. His fingers responded in kind, playing with me like I was a prize concert fiddle.

When his hand moved from my breast to my throat, I tightened, but somehow it also heightened every sensation. He squeezed, narrowing my air channel, but not hard enough to close it.

This was decadent and exciting, and my body responded in a rush of wet heat.

"That's it," he groaned in my ear. "Oh, fuck, Kylee. Cum for me!"

His orgasm hit like a wave smashing into my G-spot, and I arched into another epic release. I came for him just like I had on the boat, but I had no sound in my open-mouthed scream of ecstasy.

He released my throat and pulled out of me, spinning me onto my back and burying his face in my wetness before I could draw a full breath. He lapped and toyed with me until I writhed with my hands holding fistfuls of his hair.

He made his way up my body to claim my mouth with his. In one motion, his cock filled me, pulling another wave of heat from me. In all my years of existence, no one made love to me the way he did. He was demanding and hard, and he knew exactly what buttons to press to push me over the edge.

I grabbed onto him and rode the magic until we were both too exhausted to move. He finally rolled off of me, and we both stared at the ceiling, our breaths heavy with exertion.

We slowly turned our heads to look at each other. I smiled first, and he followed with that grin that made my insides melt.

Why the hell did your wife leave you again? I signed.

"Honestly, Kylee, I don't want to ruin this moment by talking about my ex. Okay?" His fingers threaded through mine, and he brought my hand to his lips. "Besides, I have experienced nothing like this before."

I scrunched my eyebrows together and pulled my hand from his to sign, *What do you mean?*

"You. This intensity. It's like it's going to swallow us up and spit out burned ash. I honestly didn't think this kind of connection actually existed."

I didn't think it existed either.

"So, in all the years you've been here..." He held my gaze.

I have never experienced this. It is beyond reason.

He arched his eyebrow and rolled onto his side, propping his head on his hand. His fingers traced my cheekbone and his lips pressed against mine. When he pulled away, he whispered, "Marry me."

My mouth popped open, and I blinked at him as I shook my head. *I did that once. No thanks.*

"So have I, but I've never been surer of something in my life."

I pressed my lips together. *I don't need a certificate to tell me how I feel. And I certainly don't need a priest to dictate to me the rules of engagement.*

His eyes followed my hands, and he sighed, meeting my gaze. "Just think about it. I can't go back to being just friends."

I can't go back to that either, but marriage isn't the only option here. I knew this might be hard for his Roman Catholic mind to wrap around, but I just didn't believe in the human concept of marriage. My heart would always be his, but his eternity and mine were very different.

His eyebrow cocked, and a smile played on his lips. "Are you suggesting we live in sin?"

The way he whispered it and made his eyes grow wide drew a silent laugh from my chest. He broke out in a full grin when I shrugged.

He pulled me into his arms. "I don't know about you, but I'm ready for that thirty hours of sleep now."

I pressed a soft kiss to his lips and snuggled, shifting so he spooned me.

His soft breath tickled my ear. "I love you, Kylee," he whispered.

I wished like hell I could say those words back to him. All I could do was sign them, but it seemed woefully inadequate.

AS TIRED AS MY body was, my mind wouldn't let me rest. I stared out the window, wondering how someone could love something as dark and ancient as I was. Dusk turned to night, but sleep didn't come. I lay in Alex's arms while his snore filled the room.

I gave up on trying, since my mind was constantly circling around the entire trip. The things I did wrong. The lives that were lost because I didn't act sooner. They all haunted me as much as my own actions. The cold-heartedness of killing my kin just wouldn't let go of my soul. I slipped out of Alex's arms, dressed in a pair of shorts and a T-shirt, and headed out to the shoreline of the mighty Pacific.

I dipped my toes in the water and took a seat on the damp sand. The sea called to me, wailing its sorrow for another mythos laid to rest. Warm tears burned my eyes and my throat as I searched for an excuse not to drown in the pain encompassing my heart.

I thought Alex would be enough to push away the hurt, but he had only kept it at bay for a little while. Now it came with a vengeance.

I killed my own brother.

I murdered the boy I rocked to sleep when we were young.

I watched the light fade from his eyes and his form turn to crusted coral.

It was as if Neptune had my heart in his tightly closed fists. My chest hurt from the weight of what I had done. My head dropped onto my arms as the tears came. I made no noise, but the sobs constricted my chest further, pummeling every muscle in my back with their force.

I didn't know how long I sat on the cold sand with my tears mingling with the sea. I couldn't draw a full breath, and if I had a voice, I thought I would be screaming at the top of my lungs until I blew my voice box. The injustice of what I had done viciously raped my mind, pushing me closer to an edge I did not want to tumble over.

A hand landed on my shoulder, and my heart seized in my chest, locking my breath in my throat as I jerked away from the touch. Alex's eyes met mine, and one glance at my face etched immediate concern in his face.

He dropped into the sand next to me and pulled me onto his lap.

I didn't know how to rein in this hurt. I didn't know how to survive this devastation. It was beyond anything I'd ever had to withstand. Right now, the idea of Lucifer's floggings seemed tame in comparison.

For the first time in my life, I needed help picking up the pieces.

"Shhh," he cooed in my ear. "Everything will be okay. I'm not going anywhere, I promise."

His words calmed the stormy seas within me, and the tears dried up as he continued to coo and stroke my hair, gently rocking me in his arms.

His calm confidence that things would work out wormed its way next to the ruins of my soul. A strange sensation weaseled its way into my body, creating a pins and needles effect in my limbs, as if I were finally waking from an extended and very lonely nightmare.

It took me a moment to put a name to it, and when I did, I nearly jerked in Alex's grasp. The sensation seeping into me was my heart finally finding a true home.

I had no idea what I did to deserve Alex, but right now, I thanked the gods for delivering him to me. Being in his arms felt like heaven, and for the first time since I received Fate's directive all those years ago, I dared to believe I just might have found my salvation. And it was in Alex's arms.

The End

Continue The Paradox Files with book two,

WAKING THE SIREN.

About J.E. Taylor

J.E. Taylor is a USA Today bestselling author, a publisher, an editor, a manuscript formatter, a mother, a wife, a business analyst, and a Supernatural fangirl. Not necessarily in that order. She first sat down to seriously write in February of 2007 after her daughter asked:

"Mom, if you could do anything, what would you do?"

From that moment on, she hasn't looked back.

Besides being co-owner of Novel Concept Publishing, Ms. Taylor also moonlights as a Senior Editor of Allegory E-zine, an online venue for Science Fiction, Fantasy and Horror, and co-host of the popular YouTube talk show Spilling Ink.

She lives in New Hampshire with her husband and during the summer months enjoys her weekends on the shore in southern Maine.

Visit her at www.jetaylor75.com to check out her other titles and sign up for her newsletter for early previews of her upcoming books, release announcements, and special opportunities for free swag!

If you enjoyed SILENCING THE SIREN, check out the rest of the books in THE PARADOX FILES series:

THE PARADOX FILES

A protector. A lost soul. A siren looking for salvation.

Kylee Paradox never expected to be a protector of humankind, but when hell's portals open and let loose the creatures of the underworld, she can't see any other way.

Armed with an ultimatum, Kylee has no choice but to embrace her new position as bounty hunter of the damned. Sending these monsters back to purgatory becomes her life's mission.

The only glitches in an otherwise noble pursuit are those who hold her fate in their hands. They forbid her from using her deadly siren song to lure the beasts back to the pit.

If she harms even a single innocent soul in her quest, Kylee herself will become one of the hunted.

This set includes Silencing the Siren, Waking the Siren, and Hunting the Siren

You might also like THE RYAN CHRONICLES.

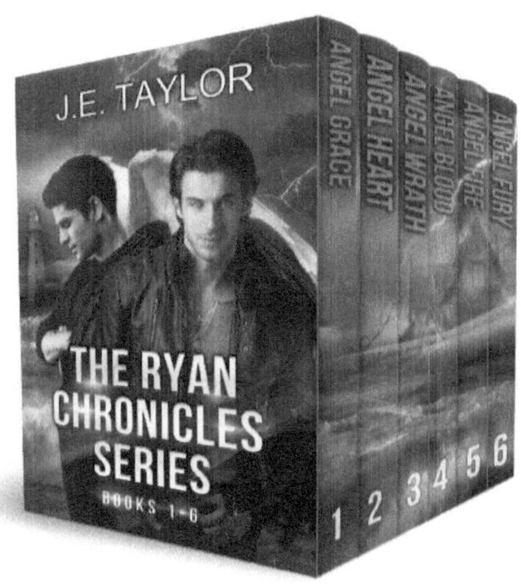

THE RYAN CHRONICLES

**Demons, vampires, angels, and the devil.
What the hell kind of nightmare do I live in?**

CJ Ryan was born with enough psychic power to destroy the earth. And Lucifer wants him to do just that.

Raised with a strong moral compass, CJ won't sacrifice innocent lives to protect his own, and that puts him at odds with the devil.

But if he doesn't give in, he and all he loves will become the target of Lucifer's rage.

When CJ gives his twin brother, Tom, a dose of
his powers to keep him safe, it puts Tom directly
in Lucifer's crosshairs.

As the final battle draws near, what will they
have to sacrifice to keep their loved ones safe?

Can they survive the devil's wrath?

THE RYAN CHRONICLES includes these titles:

CJ's Story:

ANGEL GRACE - Book 1

ANGEL HEART - Book 2

ANGEL WRATH – Book 3

Tom's Story:

ANGEL BLOOD - Book 4

ANGEL FIRE - Book 5

ANGEL FURY – Book 6

Fans of Supernatural and Shadowhunters will
enjoy this series.

Check out some of the other series set in the same world as THE PARADOX FILES.

FIRE CURSED TRILOGY

Lucifer's daughter rises.

Faith Kennedy's mother hid the awful truth from her daughter for sixteen years. Until she lay on her deathbed. Only then did she reveal who sired her daughter, and the revelation terrifies Faith.

The devil may have sired her, but he only wants her beating heart ripped out of her chest. After all, that's where her angel grace fueling her fire power is stored, and that will give him what he needs to bring about humanity's fall.

And Lucifer will take down anyone who gets in his way.

When Faith is given an ancient knife that can kill the devil, she faces the toughest challenge of her young life. She must hunt Lucifer and put him down. Otherwise, the world will burn.

But if she succeeds, she may wipe herself, and everyone she loves, out of existence.

This set includes Fire Cursed, Homecoming, and Judgement Day.

RUNNING FROM THE DEVIL TRILOGY

An escaped demon and a snarky cat face off against the seven deadly sins.

Escaping from Hell was just the beginning of Phoebe's problems. In Hell, she had a position of legend. A marquis of torture. But on the human plane, she is just another New York City destitute.

Before she has a chance to get her bearings on the unforgiving streets, Fate steps in and offers her a chance at redemption, but it doesn't come cheap.

She must bring in the demons that escaped alongside her while making sure no humans are harmed in the process. In order to do that, she needs to learn to live in the human world with the help of another one of Fate's parolees, a snarky cat named Smoke.

If it means never seeing the halls of Hell again, Phoebe will do anything, even battle the seven deadly sins single-handed.

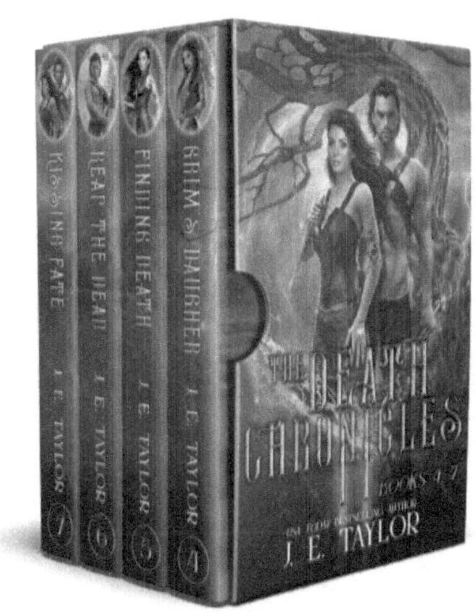

THE DEATH CHRONICLES II

Death is the family business, but not one I want to pursue. Thankfully, it's been passed down from father to son for generations, so it should skip me as Death's daughter. Then I won't have to stop being alive and can actually live my life. Right?

Well, the reapers don't agree. And neither do the angels.

One thinks I'm destined to take over, the other believes I will destroy existence. Both want me dead to match their own agendas.

I have an agenda of my own, and Leviathan who has sworn to protect me. But once my family

217

and friends start being targeted, the family business, while grim, might be the only choice I have to save those I love.

The Death Chronicles *II* includes the following titles

Grim's Daughter

Finding Death

Reap the Dead

Kissing Fate

Check out some of J.E. Taylor's other fantasy titles:

SEASON OF THE DRAGON

Monsters, trust issues, betrayal, and a near death experience.

What else could go wrong?

The end of life as we knew it didn't come with a nuclear blast. It didn't come with the deadly impact of a hurdling asteroid. No. It came in a wave of illness that swept the world with fear, and in our quarantined silence, the monsters awoke.

Leviathans, serpent kings, and dragons came forth from the bowels of the Earth. The season of the dragon began with fire and fury and ended with a new world order. One in which these giant terrorists held all the power.

When Mikhail St. Clare betrays the monsters by saving me from death at their claws, I cannot trust the last remaining dragon shifter. Not when humankinds' survival is at stake, and he had a hand in our near extinction.

The only thing we seem to agree on is our desire to annihilate the leviathans and unseat the Serpent King. Our personal futures depend on ridding the earth of these murderous overlords.

We thought crossing the leviathan-patrolled city where every corner hides a hideous death was our most lethal hurdle. But building a bomb large enough to wipe out an entire species carries its own insane levels of danger.

One wrong move and we could destroy everyone living in New York instead.

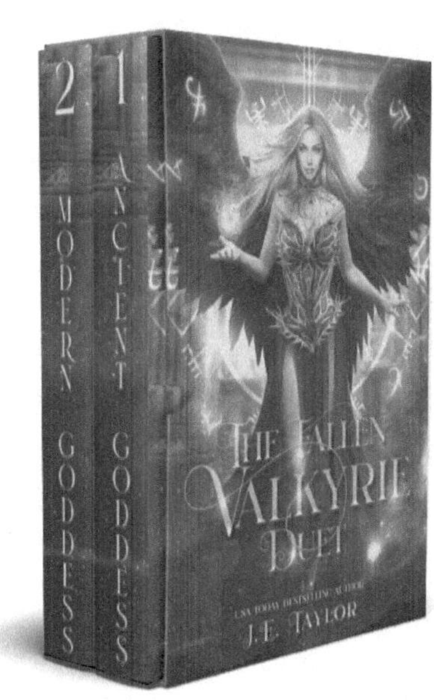

THE FALLEN VALKYRIE DUET

A fallen Valkyrie. A Fae-Wraith hybrid.

Enemies become allies to survive a god's wrath.

Odin's Order to reap an innocent soul from Earth makes me question everything I have ever known as a Valkyrie. Protecting the innocent is our basis for existing, and now I must decide. Do I blindly follow his order?

If I don't, I will be just another casualty in Odin and Thor's destruction of the realms. Anyone who challenges their rule dies a very public

221

death, regardless of their origins. And now they have enslaved Earth.

Reyfyre, a fae-wraith hybrid, and one of Asgard's enemies, has been hiding in this realm his entire life. When he finds me, he offers asylum as long as I help him kill Odin and Thor.

With everything they have done, how can I refuse?

When a bounty is placed on my head, we make the decision to leave Reyfyre's mountain sanctuary and head to New York to get lost in the city of millions. But the trek across the Canadian wilderness brings us face to face with hidden refugees, predators, and thieves.

There's no other option but to survive.

If we die, then there will be no one left to stop the callous gods before they destroy the only realm left.

But are we strong enough to take down a god?

If you like dark twists on Norse Mythology, you will love the Fallen Valkyrie duet.

THE WITCH ASSASSIN

An assassin tasked with taking out a mythical fae king...

In a realm that doesn't exist...

Mya's mission is to get in, obtain the fae king's DNA, and get out.

It should be easy with her gifts, except when does anything ever go as planned?

But failing in her line of work is a death sentence, and nothing in her training prepared her for Tavin Zorander—the most powerful Elvren to ever exist. After all, it's his family's magic that's kept his kingdom cloaked from the prying eyes of the universe for centuries.

When she finds herself at the mercy of the fae
king, Mya has a choice to make.

Does she use her darkest power, thus
compromising her mission, or should she
surrender to Tavin's desires and put his entire
kingdom at risk?

Find these titles and other fantasy, romance,
and suspense titles on J.E. Taylor's website!

www.JETaylor75.com